Don't Call Me Strong

An Anthology

Note to Readers:

When I first came up with the idea to create a book concerning the unfortunate situations black women go through, I had no idea how powerful it would be. Getting thirty black women together from all levels of society to tell their stories of where they came from compared to where they are now would be phenomenal, right? I didn't realize how emotional I'd become hearing and learning about the history of how unprotected we are as black women in the United States. Back in the day, we were expected to take diligent care of non-colored children all while being raped and beaten; just to have those same children that we took care of everyday grow up and treat our children the way their parents treated us. The history for black women has been harder than most however, it was instilled in us from the beginning that no matter what happened in our life we had to be strong.

Not just for ourselves, but for everyone in our community. I can't speak on how others feel, but as a black woman I don't want to be called strong anymore. I don't always feel strong and I'm no longer going to jeopardize my mental health by pretending to be okay all the time just to please the rest of the world. Amazing things have happened for black women within the last few decades. African American women are now the fastest growing entrepreneurs in the world at the moment.

We're taking over industries like beauty, tech, fashion, and media by storm. The sad thing is, no matter how much success we achieve, we are still expected to prove our worth to the world. Women like our Vice President Kamala Harris, and Chief Justice Ketanji Brown Jackson, will always have to defend themselves no matter how much positive change they're making. There will always be a large group of people praying for their downfall as black women in power, no matter what. The only thing they can do is ignore them and continue doing what they feel is right.

This is just something black women have been going through since the beginning of time. Overworked and underappreciated. We deal with it because we have no other choice but to push. Whether we are sick, in mourning, or depressed. We push through it with a smile on our face.

We cry in silence when nobody's watching to avoid being torn down in public. Our bullies aren't just from other races, a lot of the time it's from a man who came from the womb of a fellow black woman. There are men like the recently late Kevin Samuels who profit off publicly humiliating women. His popularity was based on the fact that he hated us black women. He was a messenger of black men. He spoke on everything they felt, he never received any backlash, just support. His death only motivated people to respect him more, despite him making a living off of encouraging men to treat us like trash. Since black women have started rising in success rates increasingly, social media has started paying attention to the lack of support from black men. I won't say it's all black men in general, there's a handful who look at us as their queens and want to do right by us.

However, it doesn't make it any better when the majority of them are against us. This book is not to complain about how we are treated though, it's to highlight how no matter what's thrown our way, we push through these different struggles. The women who are a part of this book are all quite different but at the same time very similar. It's no secret that black women are the most unprotected humans in this country, yet we're also the most needed, the most emulated, the most supportive, and even the most forgiving. All the "black girl magic" we sprinkle throughout the world comes at a price. We get challenged, but we can never react negatively to it. Unless we want to be labeled as angry, hostile, sometimes violent, and scary. Hopefully, this book can be the beginning of a change.

It's More to Life

Syreeta Martin

There were a lot of moments in my life when I wanted to break down. Moments when I would cry and ask God, "*why me? Why did he wait 14 years to be in my life? Where was he when I was a child?*" It's not like he couldn't provide for me. Even my family members were upset over his lack of support. He was always cleaned up and well dressed. I've listened to multiple conversations about how they didn't like that he wouldn't help out with his own blood.

I wasn't aware he was fighting his own battles until I was much older. He was fighting a heavy heroin addiction. We weren't close when I was young due to his absence. We were like two peas in a pod. He came to me for everything. His wisdom has even rubbed off on me, and his knowledge was priceless. His street smarts help me to navigate through life, and he never judged me.

My dad understood how I felt about men. He knew I loved making money more than being in love. He also knew that I used my sexuality to entice men to do what I wanted. I only did what I had to do to put food on the table whenever his addiction made him weak, and he understood that. As a result, I unknowingly taught myself to be emotionless towards men. I used them for whatever I needed them for.

My dad always told me, *"these niggas ain't shit."* They'll only tell me what they think I want to hear. He told me how they only care about getting what they want out of us women. Every time I let my guard down, I'd see how right he was. I needed to play the game like they do, and so I did. I was wild.

I didn't care how I made anyone feel. Eventually, I became heartless.

It didn't matter whether I was in a relationship or not, I always kept a sugar daddy on the side. My father knew the knowledge he'd share to protect me would turn me into a savage. A part of him knew his absence was a huge reason for my life turning out the way it did. He accepted the fact that he couldn't stop me, I was a scorned 23-year-old. He came back for me too late, even when he did his main focus was my brother.

Regardless of the childhood resentment, we've worked through it, he's like my best friend now. I would later make excuses for his addiction, sometimes even help support it rather than see him sick due to withdrawal. I'd even give my drug dealing boyfriend at the time permission to serve him. It sounds bad, but if you've never been in a situation where you had to watch a parent suffer through heroin withdrawals after he was kicked out of the meth clinic, then don't judge.

My life is clearly different than most. It's toxic, only at the time it was normal to me. Most of my friends went through some of the same things. Some situations were worse. When my dad got married to my stepmother, life changed for a long time. We became a family. He had a decent job, and she was one of the city's biggest boosters. Material wise, I had everything I needed. Those were the good times, but good times don't always last forever. That's a story for another day.

My mother's story was a little tragic. She was only forty when she died. My memories of her have always been painful. She drank a lot. People around me would often praise how pretty and fly she was when she was younger. They'd always tell me stories of how great she was. I could never join in. What I remember of her wasn't pleasant. She was always really sad, or a combination of drunk and angry. She loved to reminisce on old stories about my dad. She was a freshman when they met. From what I was told, my mom's downfall was directly connected to him. The story I got from other past friends was that my mom met my dad, he ruined her life, and she never got over it.

She had beautiful brown skin, light hazel eyes that made her look foreign, and a very athletic body from being on the track team. She was one of their best runners. Teenage love changed the course of her promising life. She was left with a child, a state of depression, and later suffered an alcohol addiction. Leaving me to be raised by my grandmother who did everything she could to hold her family together. I've had no other choice but to be strong ever since I was a child. The pain that I've experienced throughout my life makes me feel like I've grown numb to situations that affect me negatively. That's probably the reason I find myself having fist fights with depression ever so often. I hold so much in that it all comes pouring out at once in an overwhelming moment.

My family called me *"The Human Volcano."* I'm a calm person, however once I snap you see a completely different side. I've worked on myself throughout the years, I don't react to anything worth walking away from. I was so used to being in pain and mourning that it had become normal to me. I watched my grandmother lose six children, 3 in the same year and then her husband.

She never stopped praising God, and she continued to help raise her grandchildren as if they were her own. I watched how she just kept going and I figured that's what life was. It wasn't until I left home that I realized that there was life outside of pain. Not every neighborhood was declining from drug abuse, not every neighborhood had a rising number of tragic deaths. Some people believe in living life to the fullest, having fun, and living a peaceful lifestyle. I wasn't used to that.

I was born on the eastside of Wilmington, Delaware. My mom got pregnant with me when she turned fifteen. I was told she became a different person shortly after I was born. My dad was a popular senior and she was a very naive freshman. Eventually he broke her heart and changed her life forever. Most people tell me how pretty my mom was, all the same description, a dark-skinned girl with beautiful hazel eyes, very stylish and athletic. I don't remember my mom in the way they do. I remember her being either really sad, or drunk and partying. She became mean when she was drunk. My dad, the popular guy who everyone envied, became a drug addict. I was raised by extremely hard-working grandparents. They both grew up in Alabama. My grandfather moved to Delaware with his aunt to find better jobs. He later went back to his hometown and married my grandmother. They moved back to Delaware together to start their life as a family. My grandfather retired from Dupont, he owned multiple businesses and homes on the eastside of Wilmington, Delaware. It's a historic place for African American business owners.

My grandmother worked at the hospital. She really didn't need to; she was the type of woman that believed in being her husband's backbone. She knew he would need her in a major way one day. Together, they both built a good life for their family. My grandfather built multiple businesses around the city all with the title of *Martin and Son's*. His dream was to build a legacy for his family of six boys and two girls. All of them were taught valuable skill sets. If they would've stayed on track, this could've been a different story. In the late eighty's crack and heroin hit our community; it affected my family in a major way. My grandparents watched their children change drastically.

All their arduous work was in vain. I saw a lot of things a kid shouldn't see at the time. Unwillingly, I was educated on drug abuse early in life. I watched people I had once admired turn into different people. My grandmother never stopped praying over her children.

My grandfather never stopped trying to help them take on a legacy of his. During that time so many horrible things happened. With all that was going on in my family, I was forced to grow up too fast. The late 80's early 90's hit us hard. My uncles, who were once top athletes in the state, had skills of building homes because my grandfather taught them. My grandfather started a construction company, hoping they would end up passing it down to future generations. They were now full-blown drug addicts.

Since I lived with my grandmother, I've seen my family fall apart. By the late 90's, the AIDS epidemic hit our family hard. Half the people in the neighborhood were shooting drugs at this time. I vaguely remember one of my uncle's girls' coming to my grandmother crying. They told me to leave the room, so I decided to eavesdrop.

The lady kept apologizing. She informed her that whenever my grandmother was at work or at church, and my grandfather was working at the store, my uncle would get together with a bunch of women from the neighborhood to hang out in the backyard and get high off heroin. They were all sharing needles and sleeping with each other. As she continued to explain, I remember seeing my grandmother sitting there shocked. She prayed over the girl who was crying.

My uncle's girlfriend told my grandmother that she had contracted HIV. Everyone who was partying in my grandmother's backyard needed to get checked. I remember that day so clearly because it changed our lives. Shortly after, the lady died. Not only my family, but a lot of the people in my community were affected by the disease. In that 10-year span, my grandmother lost 5 of her children.

I told this story so you could understand the type of things I saw at an early age. Although my grandparents put in a lot of work to build a legacy for my family, bad choices changed everything. My grandmother nursed her children until they died. Imagine seeing that type of darkness, it turned me into a different person. As a teenager I was angry, I had already been through hell and back.

I stayed in trouble, got pregnant at 16, again at 18. By 20, I worked in a strip club and dated major drug dealers within the area. I made all the wrong decisions. My life was going downward, the only thing I could do to free my mind was write. I've wanted to be a storyteller since I was 9.

I'd write little plays and make my cousins perform for my grandma. We'd end up getting chastised for being way too silly. Since I was young, I have always written in my journal. At 34 I moved to Atlanta after surviving another tragic event. That's another story for another time. It's a bit much for this one chapter. Let's just say, I beat a major charge.

If I had gotten convicted, I would still be in jail today. I authored a book about it called *"Dear Little Hood Girl."* Beating that charge was the reason I changed my life and never looked back. I moved to Atlanta wanting to get into the film industry and start my own publishing company. I'm not going to lie, in the back of my mind I knew if my plan didn't go right, I'd willingly go back to the lifestyle I knew, stripping and finding myself a man with some money. That was how I always lived my life. I haven't been in a strip club since I was 20 years old. I had quit for at least 4 years at the time, but if I had to go back, I wouldn't have hesitated. At least that's what I told myself. I knew I wouldn't get back into it easily. I promised God I would change my life once I got to Atlanta, and I did.

When I first got to Atlanta, I moved in with a friend. She was a lifestyle blogger. Our first night going out together, I watched her hustle to promote her brand all night long. It was a whole new world for me. I saw women who owned their own businesses, and they were enterprising just as much as the guys. They made money just like the men did. That night changed my life. We sat at the bar and spent the night talking to some guy, his name was "T Money," and we didn't know it at the time, but he was really connected. He took the card that my friend gave him then called both of us in for a meeting the next day. He was starting a media company similar to "The Shade Room." He was looking for a team.

The hottest gossip blogger at the time was Necole Bitchie, but that's not who he was looking for. He wanted a safe place for celebrities. He gave us the address to pull up, when we did, we were stopped at this massive gate by a security guard. He called the guy and gave us permission to come into the neighborhood. I was so intrigued. I've been around celebrities before, but this kind of wealth was next level. His house was toward the back of the neighborhood. We passed many of the most beautiful mansions I had ever seen in my life, before arriving at his. When we pulled up in his driveway, I was even more surprised. He told us to pull to the back. All I saw was convict music vans lined up.

T Money was the paperman of the artist Akon's team. We were at one of their mansions to have our first business meeting. The project didn't finish that day. I still knew that was the beginning of a better life for me. The very next day we ran into a very professionally known African American producer and actress, Kandie Burrus. She was with her children in a public parking lot. There were so many signs that Atlanta was the place to help me start my journey to greatness. I worked for radio stations, small production companies, I even managed influencers and reality stars. I had never known there was a better and more stable life out there for me.

I fell in love with this life. I've started my own media company. Other people used to take credit for my creativity, I got tired of it. My company is growing fast. I help people tell their story from books to tv screens. It hasn't been easy, I make mistakes. In this industry, I still get taken advantage of sometimes, but I've been through worse throughout my life. I get to build something for my family like my grandfather tried to do and hope my children or grandchildren will keep it going this time around. My message is simple: *don't give up.* Now I get to build a legacy like my grandparents wanted for us.

It's been many times when I wanted to give up, but I never did. God is blessing me in a major way. I'm a woman who has gone through many trials and tribulations. I chased after fast money and all the wrong guys. All the things I've been through will now one day be on your movie screen. Not just for entertainment, I want girls who grew up like me to know about life outside the hoods you grew up in. You can turn your trials into triumphs.

Many people have tried to hold my past over my head to stop me from opportunities. So many men and women from my past attempt to use it against me. I don't let them get to me; my story is meant to save lives. I was once a little hood girl raised in a small city, both of my parents were drug addicts, although they didn't infect each other, they both died of aids. I was in and out of trouble growing up. I also dated a few successful D list celebrities just for money, so I guess I was a groupie in my 20's. I dated street guys, and always had some creepy older guy with money as my sugar daddy.

I once even dated a 50 yrs. old psychiatrist when I was 23. He thought he was controlling me but really, I was running circles around him. I was even in a relationship so abusive that I almost received 25 to life just to end it. My ex and his family entered my home, attempting to harm my son and me. I had no other choice but to defend us. Luckily, I beat the charges. After having to fight for my life, I needed to change my environment. I moved to Atlanta shortly after and my life changed, I never looked back. I entertained the entertainment industry with my background. It was meant to be heard, and I'm flourishing. I was able to live in a world where I wasn't in so much pain from my past life. So, you see, no one can ever hold my past over my head, one day it's going to be on big screens. You can close doors in my face because of who I used to be. I've built my own door.

This is just a synopsis of what you will be getting in the full book that will be released on my mother's birthday September 5.

Stay tuned for "Dear Little Hood Girl."

When interviewing Jackie, instantly I realized how amazing this young lady was. However, I could also hear the hurt in her voice. After reading her first poem, I feel that her words will one day heal a lot of people. Instead of writing a synopsis of what her book was going to be about, we gave Jackie an outline and let her words flow. She nailed it, I was really impressed. I believe once Jackie learns to believe in herself more, she could be the Maya Angelo of her time.

Beyond The Trees, Clouds, and Things
Written by: Jackie Davis

They say no one is born broken, but in reality
We've all been breaking since our first day out of the
womb.
I don't know about you, but for me
normality's from the 87's tragedies were planted then
and long before
simple things like,
'Sticks and stones may break our bones, but the words
will never hurt us.'

Boy were they wrong, when all along,

It's words that cut me the deepest.

Leaving a wound so revealing it could never be kept a

secret.

The amount of pressure buildup on the surface was

splitting, crackling,

breaking me into pieces.

Exposure to that type of force fractured me to my core.

When they found me, I was pleading for mercy,

bleeding, laid out on the floor.

I couldn't take the pain anymore.

I'd finally conceded, accepting my fate.

I was done.

But my ancestors had my back.

Protecting me,

they lifted me off into an ancestral realm

full of essence and love as a matter of fact,

even aided in my recovery.

Depleting rage accumulated from my collapse.

Picture a wounded black bear,

hibernating and healing for a little over 12 seasons.
Going extra hard to get strong just to prove a point,
for no other reason,
than me owing it to myself.
Nothing more and nothing less.
I was saved, bursting into a raging ball of flames.
I exploded into something mythically supreme.
From the ashes I flew back soaring from within.
Sun rays sharp and charging up my skin,
I was like a phoenix bird once my sweet voice emerged.
No one or anything could stop what was meant to sing
Beyond the trees
Clouds
And things…

I am Jackie Davis. A 34-year-old from Atlanta, Georgia. I was raised by my parents with my sister on the eastside of Georgia in Decatur. As an adult I moved into an apartment complex with neighbors who are friendly and often get together to hang out.

I grew up in an area where Atlanta was first starting to grow in music and film. It's an exciting place to live, celebrities are everywhere. Walking through malls, food shopping, you may even be going to school with someone who'll end up making it big. To a lot of people, it's a place where dreams come true, to me it's just home. I'm proud of being raised in a place where people come to change their lives for the better. I got to see people I grew up with get to follow their dreams. Even people who grew up in rougher neighborhoods experience things that most in other cities can't experience. Atlanta may seem big but it's actually small. We all know each other here. You may even find a friend who is related to a big star in some way.

Usually, the ones who come from rough upbringings, are the ones who make certain to look out for each other. The best part of growing up in a place that's so important to the culture is the experience. You get to watch your friends and associates go after their dreams and succeed. A few of my cousins were into the music industry, they've even created songs with a couple top artists.

I'm not sure what happened with their careers, but they were able to go after their dreams and achieve some level of success. Most people in the world won't get that chance at all.

Where I come from, we encourage each other to follow our passions no matter how hard life may seem. We never stop showing love and support within the community. I had a lot of dreams growing up. I played basketball, but I always said I wanted to be a physical therapist. After earning the opportunity to shadow a physical therapist, I quickly realized it wasn't for me.

It came with a lot that I didn't have the knowledge of at the time. Back then, I used to look at things as far as the salary range. It was more about how much money I'd make doing that type of job. I never really focused on the job description and the work that was required. After that, I didn't really think about a career, I just wanted to work to make money.

I lost my drive in my twenties. I lived life day by day, eventually lost track of wanting a career and chasing my dreams. Atlanta has a big party scene, that's what I wanted to focus on. I went out clubbing and begging amongst the stars. I was trying to find myself. I stopped thinking about the bigger picture. If I wasn't working, I was at a party event. I spent most of my money on materialistic things. I was a sneakerhead, always buying new sneakers, new clothes, and drinks for the club.

My struggles as a black woman are different from most women in this project. I'm a gay black woman. I'm masculine, but I was born a female. As a child, I was more of a tomboy. I've played a lot of sports since I was young, basketball was just the main one I cared for.

 I was always more comfortable in menswear. When I was young, I couldn't really explain my feelings. Now that I'm older, I think kindergarten was around the time I started to unknowingly gain crushes on little girls. It was innocent, but I felt the attraction noticeably young. I mean at that age, it was like I really wanted the other little girls to be my friend just running around, holding hands.

I was always more interested in the girls than the boys. Once I got a little older, it was confirmed. I hung around boys all the time, but I wasn't attracted to them. They were nothing more than my friends. I was starting to feel things for specific girls, I didn't tell anyone. I'm sure some people suspected I might've been gay, but most people assumed I was going through a tomboy phase.

When I got to middle school, I started to find myself. That's when I found my passion for basketball and started hanging out with females more. They were all into boys. When I did come out to them later, it wasn't a surprise, they already knew.

It was hard to tell my mom. She was more scared. She said she didn't want things to be harder for me as far as jobs and future careers. I didn't understand it at the time, but she was right. It's been a struggle. It wouldn't be as hard as it is if I were more feminine. I've talked to jobs on the phone, got asked to show up for interviews, and the looks on their faces once they see my appearance is never pleasant. They know I'm the same person they speak to on the phone, I'm just automatically judged when I walk in the building. A lot of my friends or associates that are like myself have had to settle for fast food employment due to never being picked for a better job. It's already hard being a black woman. To be a black woman that's masculine is a whole different battle. It's who I am, it hasn't been easy, not even in a place like Atlanta where there is so much opportunity. I can only imagine how hard it might be for women throughout the world.

My mom's biggest stressor was how I'd make a living as a masculine black woman. She knew I would be judged. I was too young to understand her feelings at the time, I get it now. Still, I can't be no one else but me. Although things are better than ever for the LGBTQI+ community, there's still a lot of discrimination, more if you're black.

Once I was introduced to gay clubs, I felt comfortable. I belonged. Clubbing became my thing; all ambitions went out the window. Although I was finding myself within my community, I was losing myself from all the partying.

I wasn't even spending time with my straight friends anymore, whom I grew up with.

Thankfully, I'm over that stage in my life. I know who I am, I'm comfortable in my skin. My goal is to continue to grow the business and write in other publications. I also do spoken word which I don't only enjoy, but I'm really good at. I'm finding my way, and I'm looking forward to the future.

I've found something I'm really passionate about.

I'm a writer and I own a platform, Speaking box.

I'm the only one like me in this room. With no way to navigate or gravitate.

I can't find my place.

I didn't know how or when to show myself some grace.

There was no time to exfoliate,

So much for trying to save my baby face

No time to even judge the wrinkles creating rifts into waves. I proceed as is, everyday building resilience in my veins.

When I interviewed this next lady, her story to me was like a Lifetime movie. Every twist and turn will have you on the edge of your seat. This chapter is definitely going to leave you wanting to know more. The best part of this story is that with everything thrown at her, she kept fighting. Everything taken from her, God gave back. She was allowed a second chance and built something from the ground up. Where nobody is able to take from her ever again.

YOU TRIED TO DESTROY ME

My story is a little different than most. My story could be a movie, or a dark novel from one of your favorite twisted authors. Like so many other black women, I wasn't strong because I wanted to be, I was strong because I had to be. I didn't realize how strong I truly was until my back was forced against the wall. When the person I loved the most became the worst enemy I could ever have.

I couldn't understand why at the time. Someone who knows you like the back of their hand is the worst enemy you could have. Have you ever heard of the saying sleeping with the enemy? That's exactly what I was doing, sleeping with the enemy. Only, I didn't mean to.

It wasn't until years later when I found out the true reason, he was fighting me so hard. He was dealing with his own demons. Fighting with who he was in our life, versus who he genuinely wanted to be. Looking back, I wish we would have been able to work through everything without him trying to destroy me. I lost so much.

My job, my children, my house, but most of all, I lost the man who wasn't only my husband, but my best friend.

I never realized I had the strength to endure what I went through. If you would have told me years before that I would lose everything, I would've given up at once. Sadly, there are no future warnings, and when you're in it with your back against the wall you have no other choice but to fight. I was married at an early age; I was also a mother. I went into law enforcement; I knew it was a stable career and that's what I needed.

In 2007 I started working in Corrections. My shifts were at a male prison. Working full time, I still went to a police academy in the evening. I self-paid my way through so that I could earn my law enforcement credentials. After I completed my two-year obligations at the Corrections, I started my career in law enforcement and was hired at a local sheriff's department. I worked my way to become a deputy sheriff. Later on, I received a promotion and became a detective.

I didn't leave law enforcement because I wanted to, I had no other choice. My husband at the time had become very abusive. Financially, physically, and emotionally. At the time, it seemed like he was trying to sabotage every move I made. My career at the sheriff office was progressing very quickly. He came to despise that.

He was used to the attention always being on him. He loved being the attention grabber of the family and things were quickly changing. For a long time, I was a stay-at-home wife so that he'd be able to build his career. We had an agreement, once he made it big, it would be my turn. When my turn came around, I hit the ground running.

I was back in school working full time. Then I entered the police academy. I showed my dedication and I worked hard, in a blink of an eye, I had earned my way to the top.

It feels like that's when he would start sabotaging trivial things. Next thing I knew, the physical abuse started.

First, it started with him pushing and grabbing. Next came the full-on punching. I think I was embarrassed. What was I going to do? I couldn't believe the irony. I was in law enforcement being physically abused at home.

It was kind of a slippery slope in my mind. If I said something, things would be really bad for the love of my life, but if I didn't say anything, things would be really bad for me. It was such a dark time. I didn't know what to do. We had always talked about

my career plans. He was so supportive in the beginning, but I don't think his pride was okay with how successful I was becoming to the family.
He started to isolate me over the years. I was creating a life he didn't like. Things drastically worsened. The fighting became constant. We started to despise each other. I didn't know it at the time, but that was only the beginning because once I decided to leave, he was going to do everything he could to ruin my life; And he did.

  The process wasn't easy. I was being stalked. A lot of people didn't understand how I could be "allowing" this to happen. They figured that since I was in law enforcement, I should've been able to easily turn him in. Well, my profession actually managed to make things worse.

 He manipulated everyone; he said that I intimidated him. Like I was the aggressor.

My coworkers tried to be supportive but all he did was use that against me. I remember there was one really horrible fight that we went through. I was mentally drained. I knew I had to go to work, I just couldn't bring myself together to go.

Some of the officers I worked with ended up stopping by to do a wellness check. They knew something was going on at home, I would never miss work.

They were just doing what they would do for any coworker, but that only made my husband livid. He hated that I had people around me who realized I needed to be looked after. What made it worse is that these weren't only regular friends, at the end of the day, they were cops.

Things really went downhill from there. Things were already bad, but they became awful. I felt like I was at war, and I was losing. He utilized the fact that I was an officer of the law against me. He made it his mission to get me fired and eventually he did. He was intimidated with who I was becoming. He made it his life mission to destroy me, he succeeded. To tell you the truth I don't know how I made it through but somehow despite everything, I'm able to tell my story in hopes that it may help someone today.

In law enforcement, you're not allowed to have any cases, nor can you have any protection order against you.

I lost my job because he filed a motion. He got exactly what he wanted.

Due to the circumstances, I lost my house. He refused to move out, but he also refused to pay the mortgage. I had no other choice but to find multiple jobs to pay the mortgage for a house I no longer had access to, all while paying for a new place to live. I lost custody of my children to him for a while. I didn't have a stable home for them.

He was living with our kids, in our house without me, yet left me to pay the mortgage. I had worked hard to keep the mortgage up, all while he rode around in luxury cars, booked trips, and lived his best life.

Years later, I received some closure as to what made him turn on me all of a sudden. One of my daughters told me he moved someone else into the house. Someone whom he shared a room with. My daughter spoke to me with confusion when confessing who was now living in the house. This person that he was now involved with, had been a man.

After all he did to ruin my life, I came to realize he didn't hate me because I was growing in life. He hated me because he couldn't be who he wanted to be. He never had a conversation with the children about what he had found out about himself, which is why they were so confused. I had no choice but to explain to them something I knew nothing about.

 I can't fit everything I survived into only one chapter. I wasn't prepared for the journey, but I survived it. To tell you the truth, I don't know how, somehow despite everything I'm able to share my story in hopes to help someone going through something similar. At the time, I didn't think I had the strength to get through the obstacles. This is just the beginning of me telling my story. Stay tuned as I build my brand and one day tell the full story.

Sheryl has become someone I learned a lot from. We worked on many projects together. Being able to interview her and getting to know more about her life was amazing. Through everything she's been through, she was able to live the life she wanted. Although she has a few regrets, she achieved a lot of her goals. She is an amazing person who has a lot of knowledge, and the dedication of a black woman who lives her life by helping other people.

Sheltered

Sheryl Grace

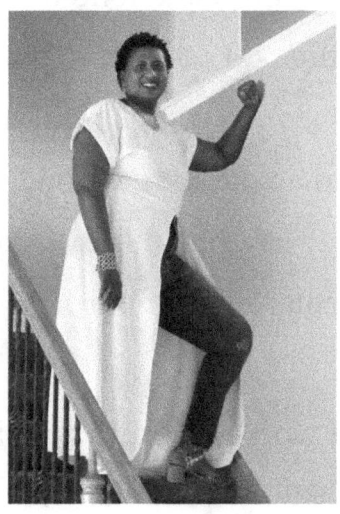

My name is Sheryl Grace. I am a proud country girl raised in the small town of St Gabriel, Louisiana. I have lived in Arlington, Texas since 1997. I moved for a better job opportunity after being laid off previously and facing the definite possibility of a second layoff.

My brother lived in Texas, and a close friend of mine had recently moved there. After hearing their reasons for going, I became fond of the idea and decided it was time for me to try new opportunities as well. It just seemed like the right time for me to start fresh. It turned out to be a good move for me and my career. I was able to fully establish my career in the mental health field.

In the past, I've worked closely with individuals who suffered not only from mental illness, but drug abuse. After working in this field for 20 years, my focus now is working with patients who are incarcerated. I became interested in the field a few years back. I felt like there weren't a lot of black people within that line of work.

Most black families don't talk about mental health. I know a lot of people who were traumatized from different situations, and they weren't receiving any of the services they needed. Our people need help from someone who'll care for their wellbeing. I was more interested in helping underserved communities. Sadly, most people don't think about getting help until they are in trouble. I knew I needed to work in Corrections.

I could've worked with people in the private sector who had great insurance. I have the background and education for it. However, the underserved needed more help.

I live an amazing life, an excellent job, and great friends. However, I have to admit that it does get lonely. I do wish I would have had children. For so long, I've waited for the right man to build a family with due to how I was raised. Every time I thought I found the right man, it wasn't.

Sometimes, I think about adopting. It's a decision that I struggle with because my life is busy. The more projects that I take on, the more I struggle with that decision because I know firsthand the amount of commitment required.

I'm also an author. It's something I've always wanted to do, even before studying mental health. I wrote two fiction books, and I'm a part of a few literary projects. Most of my projects are inspired by things I saw or people I've met. I've always had an active imagination. Writing is my way of combining my vivid imagination with life experiences. I wrote my first book in 2015. Authoring a book was always something on my list of things to do, I didn't have the confidence or any idea on how to go about it. The dream never went away. Finally, I hired an author coach to help me draft a story that I had in my head for years. I started writing and before you know it, I had created a book. It was an immensely proud moment for me and something I always wanted to do.

My very first book is called, *"He calls her Blue."*
It's a coming-of-age novel about a girl named
Indigo. From the time she was born to a teen
mother, she was abandoned by both her parents and
left in the care of someone else. Years later, the
person could no longer care for her. Her mother
had to come back into the picture, but she did so
unwillingly. She made sure Indigo was fed and
bathed. However, she wasn't interested in creating
a bond with her daughter and she was still young
herself. Consequently, she would leave Indigo to be
raised by other people, some good and some bad.
As a result, Indigo experienced some traumatic
events which would greatly impact her life.

The book chronicles Indigo's journey of self-
discovery which would eventually lead her down a
criminal path. My goal is for my books to be
transformed into movies. My upbringing was also a
different upbringing, yet not uncommon. Both of

my parents were a part of my life. I knew them well and I saw them often. Although I knew my biological parents, they didn't raise me. My paternal grandparents did, and I spent most of my time with them. Each of my parents had other children, but I'm the only one they had together. I grew up in a deeply religious household. It was Sunday School and Church every Sunday. Most social outings involved church and family. I didn't socialize much outside of school, church, and family activities which usually involved the same people. Basically, I had a very sheltered upbringing.

 The downside of it was I had to learn a lot of things on my own. Although the characters from my book and I are vastly different, I think we have some things in common. I went through a period of being socially awkward. My social skills and my confidence didn't start to develop until college and beyond. My grandparents made sure I felt loved. I wasn't really resentful of my parents but for a truly short time I was more resentful of my father than my mother.

The reason being, I just felt like he was irresponsible and passive when it came to his kids as compared to his other brothers and their children. I thought he could have at least settled down and married at least one of our (meaning mine or my siblings) mothers. He seemed to do whatever he wanted. He eventually married later in life but not to any of our mothers.

His parents were taking care of me. This allowed him to live what I considered a carefree bachelor lifestyle for quite some time. There were times that my grandparents would have to direct him to take care of some matters involving me. I don't know if he fully understood parental commitment in his younger days.

I honestly had it good because his parents were raising me, and they would make sure that he would. They didn't hesitate to inform him that he needed to be in my life and help out more. He still only did the bare minimum at times. Looking back, I'm not sure if his other children had it worse, but we all lived close by in the same small town. My grandfather made sure all of us knew each other. It's possible that each of us had different experiences when it came to my dad, but I'm not sure. I believe that at some point all of us may have experienced periods of confusion and resentment, but I can only speak for myself because I've never discussed it with any of them.

Entering the Mental Health field forced me to look at my family structure a lot. I was able to heal my resentment, because I knew that I could not help anyone with their issues before working on my own. Now, I can see the growth in myself and my siblings. I believe that is due to spiritual and personal growth in all our lives.

But I do wish that we were closer. Some, I am closer with than others. Don't misunderstand me, we love each other tremendously. If I need any of them, they are there for me and vice versa, but I wish our bond could be stronger. I think growing up in different households forces our lives to be fragmented like pieces of a puzzle with different shapes and colors but when they come together, they form a beautiful and valuable piece of art. When we are together, I see the features of my father in all of us and that gives me boundless joy.

I think in the minds of my father's other children, I received more attention and spent more time with him. But that really wasn't the case. I was in his parent's home so quite naturally when he visited them, I was there. I think my father, like so many, failed to realize the importance of being physically and emotionally present in the lives of their children. They thought as long as they were providing for our material needs, we were good. I knew in his mind and heart, he meant well. I'm grateful because I knew my father and I saw him regularly. Looking back, I realize that he did what he thought was best at the time.

As I became older, it became easier to talk to my father about a lot of things. He was remorseful and he committed to being a better father. I began to depend on him greatly for emotional support. When I decided to move to Texas, he was the main one pushing me to go. We talked a lot, and our bond grew stronger. He was also able to be there for his grandchildren. I knew that meant a lot to my siblings.

When he died, I was not prepared. I experienced an overwhelming sense of sorrow and emptiness. Especially, because his mother (and my grandmother) died earlier in the same year. It was as if the very foundation of my life crumbled beneath my feet. Through it all, I learned that we have to love our parents for who they are and forgive them for what they are not. My faith in God helped me to understand this better.

College was a big turn in my life, I went through a lot. I went to three different universities. First, I went to Dillard, I spent almost 2 years there. Then I went to the University of New Orleans. I eventually graduated from Southern University. I left the first school due to financial reasons. It was a private college and financially it was a burden on my grandparents and my father. They didn't tell me to leave, but the financial burden was visible, and I could not ignore it.

Dillard was a private school and even with financial aid, it was a strain. It was exceedingly small, smaller than a lot of high schools. It was a Methodist college. There was a lot of structure there. It was a feeling similar to still being at home with my parents. There were strict rules and curfews.

When I went to the University of New Orleans, it was a big culture shock. During my college life I was very naive. I didn't get into any substance abuse or anything like some students, I was too scared of that lifestyle. I did date all of the wrong guys. I had been way too sheltered. I lacked confidence and allowed a lot of mistreatments. It wasn't physical abuse, but I was mistreated. Even with friendships, I had friends that would take advantage of me because I was so naive. They'd take my kindness for weakness. I had to learn to speak up for myself and set appropriate boundaries. It was just something I had to learn along the way. I urged myself to figure it out.

I didn't like the feeling of being mistreated or

teased. That is why to this day, I do take part in any mocking or name-calling. Truthfully, I had to be away from my grandparents to learn life skills. I didn't realize just how much my grandparents had shielded me from until I went to college. I had to quickly figure out some things, learn from my many mistakes and experience a lot of embarrassing moments. I struggled greatly with my self-esteem and self-image. Honestly, I have emotional scars. There were some dark times. If I didn't go through them, I wouldn't be the person I am today. I can still hear my grandparents' voice saying, "you can come home if you don't like it", but I had a lot to prove to myself and I did just that. Helping people who have been through trauma has fulfilled my life. In summary, my life story has a lot of twists and turns with pain, regrets and but thankfully, a lot of healing.

At this point in my life, I'm excited about what lies

ahead. I have future book projects planned and I launched SURA Magazine which promotes and profiles best-selling and novice authors. I am now working toward bringing SURA the national attention that it needs and deserves.

I relate to Allison more than a lot of the women in the book. She reminds me of the girl of a neighbor, a cousin, a friend, someone who grew up with all the odds against them. Who made a way to survive. It wasn't always the best way, but sometimes it seemed like the only way. One thing about Allison, she doesn't look like anything she's been through. Despite it all, she was able to build a remarkably successful business. When the world looks down on mistakes she made in her past, she's able to hold her head up high because the people she has helped and the things she has done to change her life have been mind blowing.

Prison Break Coach

Allison

My name is Allison. I was born and raised in Queens, New York. I currently live in Dover, Delaware. My parents were only sixteen when they had me. I was put into the foster care system because they felt as though they wouldn't be able to take care of me at the time. They hoped to be able to raise me later on. The Butler family is whom I was placed with in the meantime. They ended up adopting me when my birth mother passed away of leukemia when I was thirteen.

My birth father fought the adoption process, he refused to relinquish his parental rights.

Unfortunately for him, I had already been with them for 7 years by the time he reached out. He lost the court battle.

Finding my biological father is something that I have been trying to do periodically, but I've never been able to contact him. Throughout my search for my father, I've found my birth mother's family. They have no idea who my birth father is. My mother died before anyone could find out who he was. When I first reached out to her family, I talked to her older sister.

Turns out, there was a lot going on during the time of my birth mother's pregnancy. She was pregnant at the same time as her own mother, my grandma. I was surprised to find out I have an aunt who is around the same age as me, just a few months older. My mother's other siblings were way older than her. By the time she was a teenager, they were out of the house with families of their own.

They didn't have time to pay attention to my 16-year-old mother's dating life at the time. It's a challenging situation for me not knowing who or where my father is. It weighs on my mind often. My foster family is the only family I've ever really known. I grew up in a house of 5 other adopted children, we were a middle-class family. My mother was a homemaker, and my dad worked two jobs. We tried our best to help our mom around the house whenever we could.

They took my adopted siblings and I in as if we were their own. Life wasn't perfect, but I'm grateful I had them. There's a lot of children in state custody who fail to get placed in a stable foster home. I was lucky enough to have a stable roof over my head.

Despite the fact that they made sure we were fed, bathed, and not out on the streets, our foster parents didn't really give us much.

They claimed there were too many of us. They made it seem as though they couldn't afford to give us nice outfits, or the newest released shoes. My foster parents were too old to take responsibility for six children the way they did. Growing up, they were strict and had a way of discipline. There was a lot of physical and emotional abuse in the home.

They didn't necessarily know how to help us through challenging times, they lacked emotional support. We weren't the only kids they had, there was an older biological daughter. Once they had died, it was her who had to take us in. Living with their daughter now meant we had to move to Delaware where she lived. Things started to become chaotic around that time.

I didn't want to be in Delaware, I hated it. New York was my home, and I was being torn away from everything I had known. My life had turned so upside down that I had gotten into a habit of running away from home. I was never able to express my true feelings to anybody. None of us really did. We basically accepted the fact that our adoptive parents were dead, and she was our caregiver now. We knew we had to move on with our lives. So that's what we did.

When I first started going to school in Delaware, I came up with my own plan to avoid being socially active. I didn't care to make any new friends. Living in Delaware was only temporary for me. Before I went to bed every night, I'd tell myself that I'd move back to New York, and that I could do it on my own. It was a time of struggle, no one really listened nor cared about anything that I had to say, or we had to say. We were children, it was like we felt we were obligated to be grateful that we had somebody to take care of us. Our foster mother was gone, we could've easily been sent back into foster care.

We barely made friends; it was hard. People made fun of us. They felt they were better than us because of where we were from, we were bottom of the barrel in their eyes. The conditions that we lived under weren't exactly ideal. It was a lot of us all under one household, it was chaotic. I needed to find a way to get out. Living in a house like that was overbearing, but under her roof, once you turned eighteen, you had to get out anyway.

By the time I turned eighteen, my plans changed drastically. I was pregnant and settled with the idea of living with my baby's father. It seemed like the best option at the time, things were okay. Until he started to hit me. I never knew what to expect.

He was hooked on drugs and became explosive at the most random times. I started to work two jobs. In the daytime I'd work at the bank, and then I'd work overnight for a news journal so that I could earn enough money to move out for mine and my baby's safety. There was even a point where I turned to shiestyness in order to get by. Whether it was writing false checks or shoplifting to get it.

It became my way of providing, I had to take care of us. There were all kinds of things I had going on, selling drugs, and a few other things you can think of in that arena. At one point in my age of eighteen, I worked in a department store. I'd have my friends and one of my sisters come in, pick out what they wanted, and once they were down, I'd falsely run it through the cash register as if they had paid. That's how I got arrested for the first time, on charges of theft. I didn't get sent to jail due to it being my first warning, but it did go on my record.

My life went sour from that point on. Having that on my record prevented me from getting a job, keeping a job, or even doing anything to make a livable wage. I always suffered the consequences of that situation. No matter how good I was trying to do, if I got hired at a job that I was qualified for, it was lost as soon as they did my background check. It caused me to believe no legitimate job would take me in. I became entangled in doing more financial crimes that flew under the radar. It only just continued to catch up with me.

At that time, it wasn't really popular for women to go to prison, especially if it was for a nonviolent offense. I racked up seven felonies over the course of time. Never doing prison time, only probation or house arrest. I didn't think I'd ever actually be sentenced. Until I was declared habitual.

This last time was different, I had deposited a check that didn't belong to me. It belonged to a company I worked for. My crime was committed in Pennsylvania, their laws are different from what I was used to. I had no idea. I walked into court thinking I'd be going home afterwards.

I was denied the opportunity to get my affairs in order and was sentenced to 7 years in Pennsylvania State Prison. I luckily didn't get federal time, but I did get maximum security because I wasn't allowed to serve my sentence in a county jail. At that time, I had two children. One was in eleventh grade, and the other in seventh grade.

At first, they stayed home with the man I was dating at the time. They started to have their own set of challenges while being there and ran away. The situation affected my son differently than it did my daughter. He ended up staying with different people on the street. My daughter stayed with her grandmother.

We've discussed it over the years, and I don't believe that they were angry at me. It was more of feeling like their life was over. My son told me that the day he found out, he just couldn't bring himself to do anything. I was all he had, and I was being taken away for 7 years. He tried to do whatever he needed to make sure he survived.

While incarcerated, I knew I was going to have to make some real changes. I also knew I couldn't rely on getting hired by a good company after already experiencing the rejection with a record. Serving a 7-year sentence for fraud was going to be the icing on the cake. I needed to make legit money in a way where I won't be rejected based on my past. I knew I needed to tap into the entrepreneurship industry.

I was determined to become successful on my own, without having to go through interview processes with people in higher positions. I wanted a life where I didn't have to work for anyone, I wanted to work for myself. So far, all I had was my license to do nails, I figured I could make decent money by starting off traveling to people's homes for individual nail services. I eventually focused on mapping out a plan to build a mobile spa I had in mind.

Once I changed my mindset, that's when everything started flowing together for me. My mindset was to start to focus on all the things that I have, instead of all of the things that I don't have. It wasn't easy at first. When I started, I was worried about the lack of money, not having any credit, and not knowing how to get any clientele. I didn't even have good products, just a few people who supported me.

I talked myself through it the entire time. First, I got started with what I had under my bathroom sink, and just put some stuff together to get by. *"Start with what you have."* Is what I kept telling myself. I refused to go back to boosting, I couldn't. Truthfully, I didn't think the business would last. I remember going through so many emotions. Being a booster wasn't easy, but I had become used to just being able to get the best materialistic things. I pushed all negativity aside and continued to push through with the nails. Out of nowhere, business blew up more than I could ever imagine.

Starting out, I got some friends together and told them I would come over and do their nails for a small fee. Next thing you know, I started to become more booked. Eventually, I was invited to an event for how talented I was. One event would turn into two and before you know it, someone I met helped me do a corporate event. I then moved up to weddings and business really took off. Once I became successful enough, I expanded my business by hiring new help and opening the building that I was so focused on while in prison.

I'm telling my story because I'd rather you hear it from me than anyone else. I remember always hearing people whisper behind my back, gossiping about my life. I learned to build a new circle of friends that match my business minded energy. Staying around people who held my background over my head with their own versions of what went on in my life isn't what I needed or wanted.

I've decided not to shy away from my story. Before you know it, I was being booked to speak on how I managed to change my life around and became the *"prison break coach."* My coaching was more about mind imprisonment. Once I changed my mindset, I changed my life. I wanted to help other people do the same. I wrote a book, participated in a

TED talk, and created a podcast telling my story. I feel free, no one can ever tell my story like me.

I'm extremely thankful to have this next lady in my life. Not only do we share the same name, but she has been one of my best friends since seventh grade. This interview was a little emotional for me. I knew a lot of things she went through, but she doesn't ever really get emotional. I could tell from the interview, the things she spoke about family, love, and grief made her feel something. When I started this project, I already knew I wanted her to be a part of it.

HEALING AND GROWING

Syreeta Fisher

My name is Syreeta Fisher, born and raised in Wilmington, Delaware. I've been working in the medical field for 28 years now. I'm educated in various parts of the industry. I started health care early on when I got accepted into a Vo tech school. It's a school that helps you get your certifications faster. My goal is to have my own assisted living facility. I want people to get the right care.

Patients should have some normalcy in their lives. I wanted people to feel safe, but independent. It's going to be a long time getting through the process, but I believe I'll achieve it. I've always loved being a caregiver. It's just something that comes naturally to me.

As I start this project, the anniversary of my mom's death is nearing. I'm hurt that the time has gone by so fast, the grief hasn't gotten any easier. I really didn't give myself time to grieve after her death but lately I find myself grieving more than ever. I miss my mom like crazy, there's so many things I want to tell her. So many things I wish we had done before she left.

I come from a two-parent home with two brothers and one sister. My parents pushed us to do anything we put our mind to. They were both blue collar workers, meaning they often worked in factories where the pay wasn't bad. Our life was rather good, or at least I thought it was. My parents had troubles that we didn't know about.

We felt the tension, but we were taught to stay out of grown folks' business. One day it was confirmed, they were getting a divorce. I was angry, I'm not sure whom I was angrier with, my mom or my dad but like any other upset child in similar situations, I started rebelling. It caused me to become a mother at an early age. At 16 I was impregnated, by 17 I had my daughter.

Throughout my life my family considered me as being rebellious. I considered myself the black sheep. Sometimes I felt like I wasn't on the same page as most of my family. We thought differently. I was less likely to be included in family events because of it.

It only motivated me to be the best me without anyone's validation. Even my siblings and I were completely different people. We genuinely love each other; we just aren't as close as my mother and I would like us to be. We're often very judgmental and critical of one another.

Personally, I felt judged in the past. My relationships and the guys I used to fall for were always a topic of discussion. I agree that I made poor decisions, I introduced the wrong people to my family. However, it was my mistakes to learn from, not for them to hang it over me. They didn't make the best decisions themselves.

We'd fall into a habit of judging each other out of pettiness. I didn't mean a lot of the things I've said, I just felt I needed to remind them they weren't perfect either. Now that we're older, I want to leave it all behind. We should be sticking together in times of loss, supporting each other. Now that she's gone, it's something I'm determined to make happen.

There's a lot of traumas in my life that I haven't fully dealt with. I'm usually the "bounce back" type, never actually healing. People always complain about the hard things they've been through, I didn't want to be one of them. I'd rather not let people in on my struggles, maybe because I don't want to put my trust into the wrong person. I've heard of too many people being wronged in that way.

I believe in love, and I love hard. Placing love within the wrong type of guys was my biggest problem. The men I attracted were needy, being with them would affect the goals I wanted to achieve in life. The trick of the devil made me feel as though I needed companionship. The loss of relationships made me feel numb.

It worsened with my ex-fiancé. His death took a toll on me, it was a lot to manage. My son suffered as well; he had become attached. He wasn't my son's father, but he did play a key role in his life. He treated him as if he were his own.

It stressed me out not knowing what to do to make everything better. How do you move on when something you've been used to for so long is no longer there? I stayed in bed for a while. I didn't have an appetite, nor the energy to stay hydrated, but I knew I had to keep going for my son. Just thinking about it now makes me sad.

I remember being on the phone with my fiancé while I was in Texas with my mother. She was going through cancer treatments, and I wanted to be there for her. We were having our regular type of phone conversation, enjoying the sound of each other's laughter. All of a sudden everything just went silent on his end. I tried to get his attention by calling his name over the phone only to receive nothing. I even hung up and attempted to call back, no answer.

A couple hours later I received a call saying my fiancé had been in a bad accident. It was all over the news. At the time, I was told he fell asleep behind the wheel. Years later, the truth that he was drunk driving came out. He ran into a tractor trailer on ninety-five. I flew home immediately to get to him. Walking into the ICU room, all I could think about was the way he looked. Hooked up to all the machines, even lost an arm. There was no life in him. It was one of the most traumatic experiences. We were building a life together, and once again I was alone. My mom, she had been dealing with cancer for some time. MD Anderson was one of the best places in America to treat her type. My mom was in treatment for about six to eight months the first time and became cancer free for quite some time. 5 years later, she was struggling to breathe when she walked. She had stages 3-4 inflammatory breast cancer. That's an aggressive cancer, the survival rate is normally slim to none. It was hard watching her fight, but she fought hard.

Being in health care for so long, I dealt with loss differently than others. I go into survival mode, although when I'm alone I still break down in tears. I keep myself buried within my work, barely sleeping because of it. Now, I'm preparing to launch my candle line. I love the different scents and fragrances.

I, myself, bought a lot of candles for my house throughout the years. Always having the idea of making my own in the back of my mind. Once I started to create my own, my children were so supportive of the idea that they suggested I put them on social media to sell. It wasn't easy, but it turned out well. It also soothed me; it was like a coping skill.

I wasn't prepared to go through the trauma, but I had no other choice. My three children and grandchildren help me stay focused on the bigger picture. I miss my mother more than anything. Not having her here to talk to me every day, or even just to sit in silence over the phone is harder than I could've imagined. I know I can push through; this is a season of transformation for me.

With faith and strength, I'll be fine. I'm doing my best to make sure my mental health is a major priority. I am walking into my purpose within entrepreneurship, rebuilding my life. I believe this is my winning season.

Sherrice's story is another story that kept me on the edge of my seat. I had the biggest lump in my throat imagining her life as a child. Her unfortunate upbringing has brought up a lot of challenges in her life but has also allowed her to work harder trying to find her place in this world. It has not been easy, but she's on the right track. Her beauty business is growing, they do different events and projects. What she's putting together will be life changing, and not just for her, for other people.

Sherrice Jones

I am Sherrice Jones, born in South Philadelphia and raised in Wilson Park projects. I'm a married mother of five, currently living in a home I purchased with my loving husband in Brookhaven, PA. I'm employed full-time as a Prevention Specialist for drug and alcohol prevention, as well as a licensed esthetician. I am the proud owner of Reelashing Out LLC. Ree is the personification of all my unique experiences; it is the name I have given myself. I have come a long way from *Tiny*.

Tiny, which is my childhood nickname, is a testament to all the things I have been. My struggles are tiny when compared to how hard I fought to become the woman I am. My parents were both very young when they had my sisters and me. My mother was sixteen when she had my oldest sister and seventeen when she had me. By the time she was twenty-two she had three daughters and an abusive husband. He would frequently beat her and accuse her of being with other men and then on pay day they would drink and party, lots of alcohol and drug use which was typical in the eighties.

This pattern lasted until we were taken in by our paternal grandmother for a while. She sought to help us, but she was unable to care for us. She enlisted the help of my father's mother and the two made an agreement that we would live with her and avoid being placed in DHS. My father's mother filed for custody of my two sisters and I, and what should have been a happy ending, really didn't get much better.

My grandmother stayed in public housing or as some may call it, the projects. She had lived there for 22 years and because her three sons were grown and lived their own lives, she was at risk of moving into a smaller unit with enough space for just her. Taking us in eliminated that risk. Don't get me wrong, I am sure that she had love for us. She would often say that she always wanted daughters to family and friends. It just seemed like we were war pawns that helped better her lifestyle.

This became clearer as the years went on. I remember how mentally and physically abusive she was. There was a lot of verbal abuse as well. She'd tell us how nobody wanted us, and we were lucky she took us in. She would reinforce this attitude by telling us that our other family didn't want to even visit us, so we became estranged from our mother's side of the family. What I learned later is that they reached out, but she made sure that we were unavailable and pretended that we were not interested in seeing them.

She beat us every time she was frustrated. She blamed us when our grandfather didn't come around, feeling as though we were the reason he wasn't there as much anymore. They had been estranged for years, before she took my sisters and me. However, when things went wrong for her it seemed to be our fault. The truth was he had another family in Delaware. I don't know too much of their story, what I do know is that although they were married and not divorced, he only popped in occasionally. It was clear he wanted to move on, he was well off. He lived in a nice house and worked a really excellent job at Chrysler. That's all I knew about him.

She just needed someone to blame for the fact that he had left her and to save face for why she was treated more like a long-term girlfriend, than a wife. She'd tell us how she regretted taking us in, and say we were only good for the benefits she'd receive. Throughout elementary school I suffered physical abuse; I looked the most like my mom. My grandmother made it known that I was the least favorite. I was bullied for my looks, encouraged to believe I wasn't pretty. She verbally admitted that she hated my older sister and me. There was colorism within the household even though we were all considered to have deep brown skinned tones.

My youngest sister, along with being the lightest of us three, was what my grandmother considered almost the spitting image of our father. She was her favorite. If you see my younger sister now, she looks more like my mother than I did. I'd always be reminded that I looked nothing like my father because he was light. I grew up listening to questions about whether he was my actual father or not. It caused me to turn against my younger sister, I'd bully her for being so loved while I was so hated.

My older sister thought differently about the situation. Feeling as though we should be grateful that we weren't sent into the foster care system. In her head, we could've been worse off and that was true. Although I understand her point of view, it still upset me. Throughout my childhood I always felt less than. Our grandmother made sure we were clean, but we didn't have many clothes. We often wore the same things over and over, sometimes the same pants all week.

There were many drunk nights where she'd beat us for no reason. She was a bad alcoholic, the only reason she stopped was because she almost took her own life in a drunk driving accident. After the accident she went into church, and it was helpful to all of us. I was in sixth grade around that time. We'd go to church almost every day. At church she was able to feed her ego and was lauded for taking in her three granddaughters and paraded us around to gain attention. Most of the physical abuse had come from when she was drunk, so her no longer consuming alcohol 24/7 meant that most of the beatings stopped. It was the heavy verbal and mental abuse that stayed.

My parents were barely active within our lives and a part of me wonders if it was somewhat related to parental alienation or their personal struggles with addiction. My dad for one was living his life, impregnating woman after woman. Today, I'm not even aware of how many siblings I have altogether. After the three children he had with my mother, he fathered four more children with another lady, a few here and there with several other ladies. Before settling to raise the last five children. I lost count around the 17th child. I was able to get connected with some of them through social media. My father didn't have a decent relationship with his mother either. There would be times where they'd talk about visitations through the state, he hardly showed up.

Our mother would make the same promises, we'd never see her. Maybe on holidays or birthdays, never consistently. This became more prevalent after the birth of my brother. However, the additional children and the inconsistency with their visits solidified the idea that we were as unloved and unwanted as our grandmother claimed.

It was like experiencing a form of Stockholm Syndrome. Yeah, she was a terrible person who treated us like crap, but as she would say, we should've been grateful that she took us in. We had gotten to the point where we believed that if we stuck by her side and behaved, maybe the church would take all the bad flaws away. We'd hope that she'd become a better person one day. She didn't…

She believed that taking us in was her good deed. We were the ones who had to accept the fact that she wasn't changing.

It was to the point where I could no longer take it, I ran away at 14. I'd start going to my grandma on my mother's side. I realized we only lived about a 15-minute walk away. They feared the neighborhood I had lived in, so I took it upon myself to find my way to them. My father would appear, trying to convince me to go back to his family. I refused; I was tired of dealing with the mistreatment.

I was the one being treated the worst, they didn't understand. Since no one wanted to listen to me, I acted out, I cut school but kept good grades. It was the worst thing I could've done. It was going good at first, until I cut school with the wrong person. We were going to her boyfriend's house; he was an older guy, and he had a friend there with him. I was a virgin. His friend forced himself on me. I didn't want to at that moment. He just didn't stop. I learned in church that my first time that was supposed to be sacred and special, only for it to be taken by rape. A part of me was stolen that day.

I ran back to my grandmother's house, hoping she'd at least hear me out because what happened wasn't my fault. Instead, I was called all types of whores and punished for cutting school. By that time, my mother had attempted to put her life back on track, she interceded and won a custody battle. She came back for me after hearing the situation. She took us to her mother's house, and she stayed too. I never went back to the abusive household I grew up in.

My mother was pretty much a functioning addict at that time. She worked but didn't completely get rid of her drug addiction. We often house hopped. She even resorted to marrying different men just so we'd have a stable place to stay for a bit. In high school I got my first job at Popeye's, at the age of fifteen. I have been working ever since. Around the time of my senior graduation, I got put out of my mom's new husband's house, after getting into a fight with my adult stepsister.

At 17, I graduated high school and was living in my own apartment. Most of the girls my age was discussing plans for college. I had no idea what to do next. The beauty industry is something I was obsessed with as a teen. After graduating I enrolled into a community college in Philadelphia. I could no longer afford to follow my dreams. I had real adult bills and responsibility. I was no longer focused on doing what made me happy, I needed to figure out what would help me survive. Someone convinced me that medical would be the best decision money wise, and I agreed. I went back to a trade school, Star Academy, for Medical Assistance training. Finding a job as a Medical assistant wasn't as easy as I thought it would be. I had the certification; however, my lack of experience was a factor.

There was a lot of depression and trauma from my childhood that I dealt with. I was now in a long-term abusive relationship. My mental health was untreated and severe. I survived two suicide attempts, first at age 10, then again at age 21. All the trauma from my past affected my future and I was determined that I would not allow the weight of my trauma to keep me from the life I deserved. After getting out of that abusive situation I vowed that I would never be abused again in any shape or form.

I got pregnant with my first daughter shortly after that relationship ended which was the inspiration for me to go back to get my bachelor's degree in business management. Halfway through school I had my second daughter and began to seriously consider again what I really wanted for myself. I had always wanted to own a business for myself. This was my foundation.

In 2015, I graduated with a master's degree in Public Health. During that time, I was working at a local center for children on the Autism Spectrum. When pursuing my degree, I had hoped that I would be able to make more of a difference. The reality was that I had invested so much into educating myself, that job satisfaction was lacking.

To make matters worse the pay didn't match my credentials and the company refused to pay me my worth. I resigned. I may have worked around 12 to 13 different jobs since 2015. I was determined not to be held in positions where I was undervalued and underpaid. None of it felt like the right fit for me.

Sometimes it was the pay that bothered me, other times it was the environment, a lot of the time I'd just felt overworked and burned out. I never thought I'd find the one right job for me, but I refused to give up on myself.

A few failed relationships later, including one failed marriage, I met my current husband while in grad school in 2013. He added two bonus sons to my family. We had our own child together in 2019 and she completed our blended family. While pregnant with my last daughter I was able to reflect on what I was passionate about in my early life.

Being a mother of daughters puts my life in perspective. It got me thinking about what kind of life they would lead. I was suffering from post-grad depression. I really liked working in the non-profit sector. However, spending long hours away from family and at work just wasn't worth the pay. I wanted to get back to my passions and I remembered way back in 2014 when I attempted to start my own non-profit in Philly. We would provide free resources and life skills, while also reaching out to help support the youth. It felt amazing to work with the at-risk youth. It was my opportunity to be the person I once needed. I was able to get in connection with more available resources.

I hosted and attended a lot of free community events, even attempted to collaborate with other organizations. I wanted to do everything in my power to give back to the youth. In the city of Philadelphia, it's more about who you know when it comes to navigating that whole grant world.

I didn't have enough connections throughout Philly at that time. Today I am still involved in nonprofit organizations. It is something that I am still enthusiastic about however, I understand that this cannot be my bread and butter.

Being business minded was something I had under my belt. Figuring out where I belonged was the struggle. I'd sell Mary Kay makeup and other equivalent items that I knew people loved to gain business experience. I also discovered that selling products like Mary Kay was about affordable self-care whether, make up, handbags, candles you name It. This was a journey I was on without realizing it since I was twenty-one.

I had time to clear my mind and reintroduce myself. I am now Ree' Lashing Out, a play on words which gives a nod to my mobile lash artist beginnings. While also serving as a platform for my hope to inspire people to lash out against whatever is holding them back from their goals. During the pandemic I was an essential worker working in the non-profit sector.

However, I wanted to empower women to normalize self-care and to throw away preconceived notions about what beauty means. My business combines my education and background in mental health as well as my life experiences and my passion for the health and beauty industry. I officially started ReeLashing Out LLC on Labor Day, 2020.

My grandmother passed away recently. I've come to bring myself some peace from what she put me through with lots of prayer and self-care. I'm still working on my mental health one day at a time. I have organized and hosted two annual mental health awareness events where people can openly discuss and receive resources and education on mental health and self-care.

My confidence is better these days. For so many years I was torn down by a woman who was supposed to cherish her grandchildren. Now I'm in an industry that helps women feel how beautiful they truly are inside and out. I know I can thrive in the health and beauty industry; I am determined to dedicate the rest of my life into making ReeLashing Out big. Isn't that ironic?

I lashed out and looked for love from unwanted
spaces
I mean there was a time
I wasn't wanted
That haunted me to be alive
To wake up
To even be
To exist and not belong
To be weak and not strong

Day in and day out being torn down by the ones
who were supposed to love me appearing strong on
the outside
Filled with rage on the inside
Refusing any help because of pride
Proud of what?
At such a young age
I was left, I was taken
I was lost, I was breaking
I held on to myself, but life scared me, I was
shaking
Often filled with confusion about beauty
Beauty is not in me
I am too dark; life was dark too.
But I had to be tough
I was told not to love my self
Why would I? Who would love me?
I said no but he still touched
Is that love? Is that beautiful?
I felt something but I can't feel
 I'm doing too much
I'm alone and too much Silence made me think
about things
Until the only noise I could hear is my own voice
saying everything
screaming inside until I could feel myself shout
Words of people I loved
telling me what I deserve, I

Appearing to be confident
But not so deep down riddled with self-doubt
Today I'm here I survived
I'm alive and I'm not what those people think
I'm not any of those things any of those words
I don't have to prove a thing
I'm me and I love me even if they didn't even if
they don't
Even if they won't. There is no more doubt. I'm
ReeLashing Out

When I interviewed Stephanie, I realized a lot of things she had to endure at an early age were heartbreaking. Her story of being homeless for years was heartbreaking, with all she went through all that she was able to overcome was amazing. Being a mother determined to give her children the life she never had seemed to be her motivation. Now, she's an entrepreneur building a legacy for her and her children. This was a hard story to tell, but how the story ended was the best part for me. Only telling one chapter of the story was the hard part. From everything this young lady had been through, she has worked extremely hard to create a good life for her and her children.

Homeless child

Stephanie Chapman

My name is Stephanie Chapman, the second youngest of four children. I was born and raised in Philadelphia. My mother's oldest two didn't grow up with us. They were taken out of the home when I was just a baby. My brother and I were raised with our mom, while the oldest two were living in group homes, eventually moving to the dad's side of the family by the state.

We had a rough upbringing; my parents weren't together. My father was in and out of jail. I'll admit whenever he wasn't locked up, he did make it his business to help out with me. He suffered from drug abuse; it was petty offenses that constantly brought him back into the system. My mother was on drugs as well, along with being an alcoholic.

We were always in unsafe situations. There was one point when we were living behind a Burger King downtown. My mother was so hooked on drugs that she wasn't protective of her children. We'd be around untrustworthy men. Men who'd turn to 4-year-old me for fun.

The first time I was ever violated was by my mom's boyfriend. We were living with her cousin when it was finally discovered that he'd been touching me. They reported him and he was convicted, then sent to jail. The whole situation was public. The sexual abuse didn't stop there, that was only the beginning.

For a while, I was convinced I was cursed. I was unprotected. It happened to me multiple times throughout my life. All the way up to age 19, I experienced date rape. School was an escape for everything I had gone through, I was a fairly good student. I even participated in an internship at Temple University for nursing. In my head, if I did well in school, I could provide a better life for my family.

The men in my mom's life were aware that she was too busy getting her fix to worry about us. It was to the point where I just blocked out what was happening. I was a pawn for sick men. It was such a traumatic time that I hardly remember how many times it happened. Out of all the times I experienced it, I can only remember four. That's how bad it was.

DFS stepped in when I was around the age of twelve. At that time, we were going from place to place, staying in shelters. I felt comfortable and safe within shelters. We weren't around crooked people, and it caused my mom to be sober. My brother was able to be a child, and I was able to breathe. Eventually the shelter helped my mother get public housing. It was nice seeing my mother get better from her sickness. I had seen so much that I had become out of control. As I got older, I looked for the love and protection that I lacked. I was practically taught to be promiscuous at an immature age, it only worsened.

When I was a teenager, I became involved with a guy who was 8 years older than me. He was the local neighborhood drug dealer, I thought he was everything. He could protect me and keep us on our feet whenever my mom spent too much money on her addictions.

It felt good to have someone that I actually wanted to be paying attention to me. For once, I chose him, he didn't force me. Sometimes I wondered why no one came to save my brother and me. By that age, I needed someone who could protect me. So that I could protect my brother.

By the time I turned sixteen, I was pregnant. Around the same time, my mother's old boyfriend had gotten out of jail. The same one who had assaulted me when I was a child. I don't know how they reconnected, but I remember all of the excuses she made for him. How it was learned behavior, she'd tell me he was a victim himself.

I was shocked that she let him move back in the house without telling us. She didn't care about our safety. In her addiction, she was always selfish, her feelings always came first. At this point, I would've rather been on the streets than with her.

If it weren't for me getting pregnant, I probably would've stayed. I didn't leave right away. I was seventeen when I had my daughter, I still had to go to school. Leaving her home with my mother and her boyfriend made me so nervous. Finding out my baby was a girl was the scariest day of my life. I knew I couldn't stay there for too long. I needed to protect my daughter the way my mother failed to protect me.

It didn't take long for my mom to relapse once her boyfriend came back into her life. The checks I'd get from the state to help take care of my daughter were going to my mother. Since I was underaged, all the checks had to be addressed to her. Instead of giving them to me, she'd spend it on their addiction. Causing my daughter to be out of pampers and formula occasionally, I knew I needed to leave, I was fed up.

First, I stayed with my grandmother (my dad's mom) for a while. That didn't really work out for too long. I decided to move into a teen shelter to help myself become more responsible for my baby. I found a shelter for teenage moms. They catered to teen moms, helping them with resources, classes, and eventually homes.

We stayed in transitional housing for a while after leaving the shelter. I was eighteen and had been stable enough to return back to school for my 12th grade year. I went to Thomas Edison, I felt like my life was back on track. Things just seemed to for once, move in my favor. I was able to be comfortable with my child.

I was now ready to start dating. I was no longer with my daughter's father. I met another guy who was also older than me, I was around nineteen. During our date he slipped something in my drink, took me back to his home, and raped me. It affected me so badly; I had thought experiencing that was over. I blamed myself. Telling myself it was my fault for putting myself in that situation. I vowed it would never happen again; I started being extra careful around men.

The only regret in my life was leaving my brother behind. I carry a tremendous amount of guilt behind it. My mother's decisions affected him the most. I'm not too sure what his upbringing became, but I know as an adult, he faces a lot of struggles as well. My mother wasn't good at being a parent.
All four of us siblings have reconnected, but no one knows the other's story. We don't go too deep in talking about how my mom affected us. That's something I'd like to work on, healing together. Our only bond is surviving after all we've gone through. I want to know more about their lives and be a family.

In the years of 2011 and 2012, my mom did get clean. She gave her life back to God. In 2013, she got infected with aids and suffered from cirrhosis of the liver. She passed later on in that same year. On the other hand, I have an amazing relationship with my father.

There was a time where we even lived together for a while. I had lost my place after going through some trials and tribulations. He was stable enough to offer me help. He wasn't there when I was a kid due to being in and out of jail, but as an adult he has been there every way he could. Whenever he wasn't working, he was helping me with my children, they have a great connection.

Eventually, with his support, I got back on my feet. Unfortunately, now he's back into his old habit of using drugs. We still see him from time to time, he still tries to help and stay a part of their lives. I'm praying his sickness doesn't get the best of him, and I'm hoping he fights to save himself. He's the only parent I have left.

I am now a hard-working single parent of two. I own multiple businesses. Ruth Printing, named after my mom. I'm a yoga instructor, wellness coach, and also in nursing school. I receive a lot of support from the black women around me. I'm doing this for my children. I've always told myself that I would make sure they have a much better life than myself. And I'm just getting started.

After interviewing Onori, tragedy struck in her life. I want to make sure we all take the time out to pray for Onori and her husband as he gets well. As you will see from her story, this couple has been through a lot together. We want to wish them better days. Onori has been a tremendous help with this project, she recommended 3 women who had amazing stories.

Outgrowing your environment

Onori Ajong

My name is Onori Ajong. I grew up in North Philadelphia in the Germantown area. I now live in Sharon Hill, PA. Growing up, I lived in a two-parent home. From the stories my mom tells me I was destined to be an entrepreneur. At the small age of three, I was trying to make and sell my own baby wipes. No one was surprised when I started my own business as an adult.

High school was great for me. I took childcare classes because I always liked helping people. It's always been in me to be of service to others. What I did is, it wasn't something that I planned to do as a career. Teaching was practically in my blood.

My father was a science and math teacher. When I was younger, I'd play with his books and pretend to be a teacher as well. The type of teaching I do now isn't the same as my dad. My classroom looks a little different than your average school. My classroom was in the gun range. I'm an instructor, teaching people to protect and defend themselves. I'm also an agent for the State of Pennsylvania, I do private executive protection work. Higher people hire me to be on the premises for a certain number of hours to defend a property. I've worked for celebrities, high profile clients, and at big events. I did CNA work before I switched over to the line of defense and protection. It was suffering through a home invasion that made me want to get into that line of work.

When you've outgrown your neighborhood, you know that is when it's time to leave. Especially if you're growing financially and still living in the same messed up neighborhood. No matter how much you try to protect your money, you become prey. People will notice, and most won't be happy for you. I learned that the hard way.

I didn't pay attention to the signs because we were too busy building a family. It wasn't until the day my husband left, and someone tried to break the window at the back door. They cracked the glass, but we had a security bar up. I called 911 and when they came down to the scene, I let them know what happened. They told me something that day that I didn't really pay attention to at the time. They said the people who broke the glass that day would most likely keep coming back until they get what they want. I was 7 months pregnant at the time.

For us, I think the neighbors were keeping a close eye. The payoffs of our hard work had begun to stand out. The place that I was raised in became a danger to my family. I wasn't rich or famous, we were regular people who worked extremely hard. My husband was a truck driver who made a good living. At the time I was pretty much at home on maternity leave.

What I learned later is they watched us upgrade our lifestyle. They saw the cars both me and my husband had parked out front. Other than that, I'm not exactly sure what else. We never found the people who attempted to break in. It was just a scary situation for a while, but it gave birth to the new me, and changed my life forever.

It was months before the next incident, this night was different. I had just given birth to my son three months before. My husband had just pulled out the driveway. It was the day before Thanksgiving, around eleven at night. The intruders tried to enter the house through my second-floor window.

When I realized what was happening, I called the cops.

This time around, I was licensed to carry a firearm. All I could remember was what the cops warned before, the intruders most likely were paying close attention to us and would come back. They did, and this time they were boldly breaking in. I was no longer pregnant; I was now a mother, and I would do anything I could to protect my baby.

I laid the phone down and went into the room where I had my firearm while they were still trying to enter. I picked my firearm up and shot five times out the window. When you go through a situation like that the adrenaline starts to kick in and your highest level of training and you go into a tunnel vision. When I shot, everything was moving in slow motion. All I saw were flashes.

After I shot it took the police about 10 minutes to respond to the scene. Once they arrived, they chased the suspects down to Philadelphia airport. They couldn't catch them, so they turned back around. There was glass and blood all in my backyard. When I heard they had gotten away I didn't feel safe.

I wasn't fully trained to use the firearm during that situation. I just knew to point and shoot. Getting my gun license became my main priority afterwards. It's what led me into the business I'm in now, I didn't have any of this available to me.

I started suffering from anxiety. I didn't want my husband to leave the house. In fact, I told him that if anyone needed to work, let it be me. He could just stay home. Being left in the house alone was causing me to become scared and paranoid, I couldn't take it.

We were still in the neighborhood for a while, my husband put bars on all the windows and new locks on that door. I made sure the house was secure. We were planning on moving out of the city of Chester. We had already known there was a possibility they could come back a third time. It also didn't sit right with me that even after the shots were fired, no one called the police.

The police told me the only call they received was from me. They only heard the shots because I left the 911 dispatcher on the phone. I couldn't live in a neighborhood where the neighbors didn't look out for each other. They all knew I had a newborn son. Not one person called to report shots fired. No neighbor approached me to make sure I was okay. It was crazy to think that's how life would be. I couldn't even sleep at night. Even if my husband went to the store, I was anxious. It took us 6 months to move out. We found a home, in a better part of PA. Charming home, on a quiet block. I was able to breathe, the stress was gone.

As far as my career, my husband pushed me in the direction. One day he suggested being an agent in the state of PA. He knew of a few people who were in that line of work. I was interested in the proposal. If I was going to ever have to defend my daily or property again, I needed to be an expert.

In the state of Pennsylvania, when you first get your firearm and become licensed to carry, they don't require you to do any training. When I entered the range, I was the only female. Once I did all my training, I obtained a lot of work as a black female. We are really needed in the industry. We are high in demand.

In 2018, I created my own range day called "Ladies night" after experiencing what it was like to be the only black female within my unit. It was hard enough being in a sexist environment; my skin color only made them doubt me more. I refused to work in a space like that. I needed to be comfortable. I started doing these events for Ladies night with the owner's wife from the gun store. We'd introduce females to the gun range, getting them comfortable. I contacted Fox news so they could come out and do a story because of the rise in violence amongst women in the Philadelphia and surrounding areas. When they came out to do the story, Fox news only wanted to report on the female self-defense movement. When the story aired the owner of the gun store was mad because they didn't feature him.

Once aired, the owner started to slander my business and me. He thought he could push me out.

He didn't like that I was getting so much attention. He'd make false claims, saying I was a scammer, I didn't have any training, I don't know what I'm doing etc. He did everything to try to tear down my character and what I was building. All his bashing only made people support me more. I didn't understand his anger, his wife did get coverage on the news.

Regardless of his slanter, I remained professional and focused on my work. My clients took it upon themselves to fight for me. I teach the ladies everything they need to know. How to get a license, legal insurance for your firearms, and the training aspects. I'm a certified instructor so my license is recognized all over the United States.

After that situation, I saved up for my own store. I was able to offer more services to my program at the range. The gun range I use in Philadelphia is amazing.

There's been a lot of crimes against women, especially black women and I want to do everything I can to teach women to protect themselves. I had to be strong even when I didn't want to. I had no other choice but to protect my family from harm's way.

Interviewing Rebekah McDonald aka Mz. Becky was a treat for me. Seeing someone accomplishing so much at such a young age was an inspiration to me. A few years ago, I worked with Mz Becky for quite some time and what I like about her is her energy. She helped me with this project. Out of the thirty women, she recommended at least 10 women and 5 signed up to be apart. Mz Becky and I have so many new projects coming, I just want the world to know how thankful I am to have met this lady. She has been a light in my life.

Growing Up Fast

Rebekah McDonald

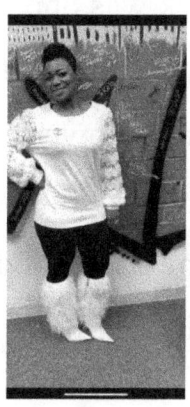

My name is Rebekah McDonald. I was born and raised in Chester, Pennsylvania. I grew up pretty fast, pregnant at 13, and birthed a baby boy at age 14. Most would think that's a lot of responsibility for a newly turned preteen, but the truth is I had been taking care of children since I was in the second grade. My mother was diagnosed with lupus when I was seven.

Some things we forget about our childhood, but some things stick in our mind forever. My mom telling us she was sick was one of those days I will never forget. I remember how I felt right there in that moment. She sat us down to inform us that she had an illness that she may die from, one day. She told me I'd need to be strong and help take care of my little sisters in place of her.

My caregiver role started before my mom even passed. From the time I found out she was sick I had a heavy weight on my shoulders. Making sure my siblings were taken care of, and always worrying about keeping them and my mother safe. Thinking back on it, I realize I had a lot of pressure on me at a young age. I shouldn't have ever had that type of pressure on me, but it's common for the oldest child when you come from a household of an ill parent.

Being a caretaker most of my life is probably why I became a nurse. I literally have been a caretaker most of my life. My father was a Vietnam Vet, he had his own issues, but we stuck together as a family. We loved each other. I just had a lot of responsibility, it made me grow up fast.

I got pregnant when I was in 8th grade, and I had to drop out of school. Not only was I taking care of my family, but now I had the responsibility to raise a child of my own. I wanted to go through with an abortion. My mom was a Jehovah's Witness. She nor my father believed in aborting a baby. They'd say, if I was grown enough to lay down and make the baby, I was grown enough to raise it too. Things didn't work with my son's father. After the baby, I wasn't as confident as I had been before. All my friends were going into high school to experience their first year and I was now a single mother who dropped out of high school. Although I suffered from weight issues, I was secure with myself until the baby.

. At the age of 16 I got my own place. I had my own car and worked a full-time job as well. Shortly after, I started dating an older man. I always dated guys way older than me. Being overweight and looking older than I was, most guys would believe me when I'd lie about my age. He thought I was twenty.

I thought he would just be some older guy I messed around with. We ended up really liking each other. We were in a relationship for a long time before he found out how old I really was, and he wasn't happy.

Although I was enormously proud of my first apartment, I eventually got evicted for owning a dog, ignoring the no pets allowed rule written in the lease. I was mature for my age, but I was still young, sometimes my mindset matched my age. When I got evicted, I was eighteen, and in school for phlebotomy. I then enrolled myself for the first-time home buyers program. That was one of the best decisions I ever made. Getting evicted turned out to be a blessing in disguise. I became a homeowner at age 19.

A person who is really important in my story was a lady named Carol Quattrociocchi, she was a realtor. She was a Caucasian lady, and she liked me. She was adamant in making sure I finished the program. There weren't many people as young as I was looking to buy a house, it became a big deal. It was a major accomplishment.

Personally, I just felt like I had no other choice. Since I had gotten evicted, I had been renting a house. The owners had told me that with the rent I was paying, I was better off buying the house. Back then I was only making nine something an hour. The first-time home buyer program helped me start out with a lease purchase.

They gave me up to 12 months to purchase the house or I would have to leave. I made sure I kept my credit together because I learned that was important. When I got my taxes, I left the money in the bank and didn't bother to touch it. The tax return was about 6800 and I was responsible enough to save the money.

I knew I had to make sure I bought my home. I will never forget it. In October, I went into settlement. I had done everything required of me. I remember penny pinching. I still had other bills, but most of my money had to sit in the bank. They needed to see that I could save money, or they'd deny me a loan.

A few banks wouldn't even take me on because of my age. Being so young considered me a "risk factor." Looking back, I probably could have sued them for age discrimination. Carol found a company that would be willing to finance me. They wrote the check and gave me a mortgage.

Carol was so invested in me, and I appreciate her deeply today. There was one crucial time in my life when she did the most heartwarming and loyal thing anyone had ever done for me at the time. During closing time on the house, I was about 1100 dollars short. We were seated at a table of four white men. Carol stayed by my side throughout the entire deal. I was the only black girl there, along with being the youngest in the setting altogether. Just being in the environment was confusing for me. It was like sitting in a classroom not knowing what's being taught, but somehow all your other classmates do. When the man asked for the money, I froze. All I could do was fight back tears; I didn't have any extra money.

For a minute we sat there in silence. Until Carol went in her purse, pulled out her checkbook, and wrote the price down. She told the man to give me my paperwork and informed me that I could pay her back when I was able. I cried that day. I was taught to never cry in front of people, but I cried right there at the closing table.

I went to the closing, Halloween of 1999. It was celebrated in the newspaper because of my age. They came out to my home and took pictures of me with my son. It was a huge moment. My mortgage was 725. I had a three bedroom, 1 and a half bath, townhouse in New Castle, Delaware. I was really proud of myself.
Later, I enrolled into nursing school. I had to quit the first year when my mom's sickness sent her to the ICU. She almost died; she even went coded one night. As she got better, she stayed in rehab for almost a year. I couldn't focus on anything else but my mom. School was on the back burner. After my

mom went through a hip replacement surgery, I made the decision to leave school permanently. When my mom got better, I went back, and my schedule became the same. School on the weekdays, double shifts on the weekends. At the time my boyfriend, who is now my husband, would keep my son while I finished. I struggled because of how much learning I missed out on in school after getting pregnant. I taught myself and really buckled down and learned.

In the process of going to nursing school, my electricity got cut off. It was off for a few months. I would take my son over to my parents' house every night to get a bath and eat.

When you are from the hood you know how to survive when things get rough. The electric was off, not the gas so I was able to boil water for myself and pour it in the tub every night.

I didn't do it with my son because I didn't want to risk burning him. My parents didn't realize what was going on for an awfully long time. My son knew better than to tell them. I told him I needed to figure it out on my own. They had their own problems.

At this time, the electric bill was up to 1400 dollars. I couldn't afford to pay the mortgage, electric bill, gas, and still have the money to go to school. I told my parents at some point.

A little after I told my parents, I ran into an old coworker who once owed me money from 2 or 3 years before. Honestly, I didn't think anything of it. We had been catching up when she randomly gave me the money, she once owed me. I had three hundred saved by that time, along with money my parents demanded I have. I was able to get the lights back on.

After that I finished school and got a job making good money. By that time, my boyfriend, Timothy McDonald had moved in. Things were going well, but it was hard for him because he was used to being in the streets. We both wanted a better life. Now he had a job as a drug and alcohol counselor with the State of Delaware. I stayed with the man for 26 years. We had a conversation after he found out my true age, I could have gotten him in a lot of trouble. Being dishonest with him put a hardship between us. My parents were bothered when I told them how old he was but all the women in my family married older men. My grandmother married someone who was 20 years older, and all of my aunts have married men much older than them. My mom is just 2 years older than my dad. I was happy and I didn't feel like I was missing anything with people my age. We were building a life together and we are still together happily with two children ages 14 and 27, and two grandchildren.

The biggest issue we had was when I decided to get weight loss surgery. My weight has always been an issue and I needed to get the surgery for myself. He struggled with the change. At that time, I was doing what I had to do for my health.

You will read the full story about that in my next book. I will say this, if you're not happy with yourself, or you need to make some life changes for health reasons you may have to make those decisions by yourself. We did go through some issues, but we made it through. Stay tuned for the full story in my next book.

I also have a cookbook, *'Cooking with Bariatric Barbie.'*

Interviewing Rasheedah was like taking a master class on faith and success. Her story not only had me on the edge of my seat, but it motivated me. When life threw her lemons she made the sweetest lemonade, every single time. Her amazing personality and faith in God have been a tool that she used to have a happy and successful life. It hasn't been easy, but she did the work.

Faith And Favor

Rasheedah

My name is Rasheeda M. Lee. I was born and raised in Chester, Pennsylvania. I'm the owner and operator of 'Rasheedah's Exquisite Hair Designs' as a beautician of 26 years. I've also owned 'Sanai Dior Ballroom & Wedding Chapel I & II' for the last 7 years. All along with being a minister of God for twelve wonderful years. I am the visionary of

Sisters Growing Strong Ministry. I'm proud of my accomplishments.

I come from a very close-knit family, I'm the oldest of 3 children. My mother and father were 16 years old when they birthed me. We grew up in the Islamic faith, religion was especially important to my parents. Over the years of my life, my father was an impressive barber. He was a talkative and funny man, always standing up for what he believed in. Satan found his way to attack his life by tempting him with drugs at a young age.

He fought that addiction for years. My mom had to raise us by herself. Having children while still in high school forced us to move into public housing. My mother showed my siblings and I what a good life looked like. She did her job so well that I hadn't even realized we were on low income. She worked as a waitress most of her young adult life. While raising us, she didn't have the qualifications for a high paying job. She still made sure we were well dressed, and everything we wanted or needed, we received. I could remember my mom receiving so many tips from work to provide for us.

She'd save it up so my sister and I could get into the youth dances. Life was easy back then, but once I was older, I realized what I thought was good living was really a struggle for my mom. She was making ends meet. I can recall asking my mom if she wanted to move from low-income housing. She was afraid because she lived in that system so long. I encouraged her to let me show her that she can buy a house.

My sister and I worked together so we could move our mom out. My mom was so happy to contribute to owning her own home, she went right to work in fixing it up. I was only nineteen at the time and doing well as a stylist. I managed to make good money at a young age. I had saved a lot of my money by doing hair since I was fourteen.

It was a really good feeling to be able to help my mother in that way. Although we lived on low income all my life, my mother was responsible. Responsibility is something she instilled in us early on. I remember watching her organize her bills on an envelope every week. She would always remind us to save, keep up on our credit, and make sure we always have car and life insurance. These were things she taught us at young ages.

Watching my mom work hard to make good money impacted me to do the same thing. Her and my father instilled business and work ethic in me. They planted seeds in me that have produced a million times over. My sister, brother, and I were so used to watching our mom hustle that we adapted to it.

When I first started doing hair it didn't take long

until I blew up. I am an incredibly talented and popular stylist.

Once I got a little older, and bigger in the hair world, my mother warned me that when I open my own business, it will have to be by myself. She'd tell me to make sure I knew how to run my own successful business before allowing someone else to profit off of what I started. I listened to everything my mother taught me. Her street smarts and wisdom actually contributed to my success. One major thing that always stood out to me about my parents was their faithfulness in religion.

Religion has always been a big part of my life. My mother was raised in Christianity, she converted and dedicated her life to Islam after she had met my dad. She found her original faith again once they separated. We went to church with my grandmother. I was never eager to be in the ministry, but I knew God.

The older I got, the less I attended church services with my mom. I found my way back in my early twenties. When I joined church, I felt like everything about my life was different. My eyes began to open to a new direction. My spirit remembered what I learned as a child, and I loved it. The streets and wildlife called my name, and I would straddle the fence with church and the world. Eventually I stopped going to church around 26 years old. I tried to find every excuse because I didn't want to go. Trying to blame my mother for past situations as a reason to not be there.

Back in my fifth-grade school year, my mother sent me with my aunt who lived in Delaware. She decided that I'd stay in Delaware during the week for school, then I was to come back home with my mom on weekends and vacation days. My aunt only had one child; she didn't want her daughter to be alone. She also knew it would be a more stable environment for me, Chester was wild at the time. I packed up and moved to Delaware which wasn't far from Chester. I went back and forth every week from fifth grade to 7th.

I was told to stay out of trouble when running the streets, instead I ended up losing my virginity within the first year I moved to Delaware. My cousin was older than me, she was in her 9th grade year while I was an 11-year-old, barely in middle school. I tried too hard to fit in, I wanted to do what the other children were doing, even if it meant stepping out of a child's place. My aunt worked a lot, leaving me home alone very often. I became very promiscuous; I was now aware of a sensation that I didn't want to stop feeling.

Even though my mother sent me away for a better education, my innocence was being destroyed. It wasn't anyone's fault because I knew how to make the right decisions. I just wanted to do what my friends were doing but didn't know that it would hurt me later. My mom assumed sending me to Delaware would benefit me but all it did was backfire on her. She didn't send me there to be grown, she sent me there to get me out of a bad environment and to get a good education. Moving to Delaware was supposed to save me from falling onto the wrong path, all it did was speed up the process. It never changed who God said I would be. Eventually, my mom brought me back home. By this time, I was in 8th grade, I had already been fast from my time spent in Delaware, it just never got any better. I started dating drug dealers. I was in the mix so bad that guys would be in the streets shooting over me. One guy I dated went as far as to put a gun to my head because he didn't want me to leave him. It was a lot to deal with, I had become what my mom tried so hard to keep me from being.

I was a cheerleader throughout my entire high school years while doing hair on the side. I had also gotten a job at Rally's in ninth grade. I still managed to be heavily into sexual relations. Guys noticed me more because of how independent I was. I was an attention grabber. I always had to defend myself physically due to being involved with street guys who'd entertain multiple women.

During high school I did hair at my house, it became a chill spot for a lot of my friends. Whenever we had enough girls there, boys would start popping up. There was good and bad that came with being popular. I made money at a young age, which kept me busy. However, it didn't keep me out of trouble with being promiscuous. By the age of 13 I had my first abortion. My mother was not happy, she didn't believe in abortions. She just wanted the best for me.

My life started changing when I went to college. Everything was different. My mother was young, she was around thirty-three when she dropped me off at Temple University. I was going to get my degree to be a physician assistant. My roommate was attending college to become a physician.

We were close at first, we were just from two different worlds. She was in school to study medicine. I was always at the school parties, or out doing hair while she stayed focused on her schoolwork. Seeing how motivated everyone was in that environment made me feel out of place. I was surrounded by higher achievers; I didn't know how to be like them.

Eventually, I became depressed. I was so overwhelmed, I wanted to commit suicide. I was only eighteen, it was my first year in college. The guy I was dating at the time stopped me from taking my life. This guy wasn't like anyone I dated before.

I was used to street guys, but my life was changing with him. He was a Christian. Due to my mother turning back to Christianity after she separated from my dad, so were we. He had asked me to marry him my first year of college. Everything seemed good, but I was very overwhelmed with all the changes. Although he was in church, he used to steal a lot. He was what we'd call a clepto. Later we moved in together. That's when things got bad. He wasn't the man he made himself out to be. He was into credit card scams, he even had stolen items come to our house.

He started bringing girls into the apartment whenever I was in Chester doing hair. The cheating got so out of control; I became depressed once again. I worked so hard to change my life because I like the difference between religious men and a street man. However, I didn't realize how emotionally drained I was until it was almost too late. Thank God that I had a mother who listened and cared about me because I wouldn't be here. I planned to jump from an area near Lincoln Drive and commit suicide, all over a man.

Afterwards, I moved out. I needed to work on myself and heal. It was a dark time for me, but I made it through. I haven't felt like that since. I've learned to cope through hard times, and not run to the thoughts of taking my life. It seemed like after that situation every man I dated cheated on me. Maybe it was the type of men I'd choose. I still have many talks with God about it today. I feel as though it might be my karma for what I helped put other women through while being in a relationship with their husband when I was younger. Even being divorced and then remarried, I had to deal with my next husband being unfaithful. I felt like what the bible says "you reap what you sow" was happening in my life.

I'm a changed woman but my karma has caught up with me for all the problems I caused in past relationships. I've learned to pray my way through it. I no longer allow the devil to talk me into attempting to end my life. Once I reached the age of nineteen, life started to really get better for me. I focused a lot on being an entrepreneur. In 1996, I worked with a guy who owned a barbershop. He allowed me to rent a space for my hair business. I made so much money that I came to the decision that I wanted to buy my own building rather than rent a chair. It was a smarter decision for me to open up my own salon. I wanted to buy my mom a house, it was time to step things up. I sat down with different realtors and asked them how to purchase a home and advise me on opening a new salon. It shocked them because of how young I was. Once they realized I was serious they were willing to help out.

I dropped out of Temple and went to Talent Academy Cosmetology School so I can have all my credentials. Afterwards my uncle helped me get my Cosmetology License. I opened up my salon and hired my mom to work there for me, I offered to pay her the same as her job. Eventually I paid her more for helping me build my business. She was willing to leave her job to work for me, we worked together for 16 years.

I'm proud to say that she has never worked another job since she worked for me. The first day I opened my door she believed in my vision, and we made it happen. I rented the building for a year and half then I leased it to purchase two years later. I paid the building off within 3 years. While I thought things were going well, I was slapped in the face when they unexpectedly took the building back from me. They informed me that my lease to own contract was null and void after they got a lien on the property. The owners had gotten a loan on the building and neglected to pay it back and I was no longer able to purchase the building. That crushed me because I took all my hard-earned money to renovate that building with no loans. My lawyer didn't see that in the clause. The building was taken from me after I paid cash for it.

I was devastated. All I could do was turn to God, the God that I abandoned when I went to college. My friend invited me to a church service. I wasn't sure if I should go at first, but I found myself making time to get there.

We went to Philadelphia to hear Pastor T.D. Jakes' sermon at the Liacouras Center.

It was seven other friends that went as well. I arrived later than everyone else. A Minister named Paula White was speaking as I looked for a seat. What she said caught my attention. I was the only one standing up, when I turned to look at her my heart dropped.

I knew she was talking to me. "You're about to give birth to triplets, it's about to happen right now." I will never forget it. I was sitting down at this point. I told my friend she had to be talking to me.

I didn't know what the Holy Ghost was at the time, but I felt something in my spirit move. When I left the service one of my good friends called to inform me that we found a building down the street from where my job was located that had been for sale. I went to see the building. It was three buildings in one, perfect for me. The only thing I could think about was Minister Paula's words. I'd be birthing triplets.

Birth isn't always related to babies, you can birth businesses too, is what I said to myself. I called the realtor and received a call back from him within 24 hours. I got a tour of the full property; I then made a deal on the building and paid it full out in cash three weeks later. I'm still in the same building today. Three buildings for one price.

I was in awe; I knew I had evolved. I began to realize the favor that was on my life. Although she was speaking to the audience, the message was meant for me. I was 24 years old at the time. I had the property for a year, and I didn't begin construction because it was so dilapidated, I just paid taxes. The next year I started getting work done on it.

My grandfather saw my vision and he executed the plan. He was an awesome contractor and builder. He made my dream into a reality.

I have been in that building for 18 years now. So much started happening after purchasing that building. I got married, had my daughter, then I bought the house that I still live in today.

At first, I only used the building for my salon, and I rented the other side for a nail salon. I hadn't done anything else with the other sides of the building. Before my mother passed in 2011, she gave me one last lesson to learn. She told me to allow the other parts of the building to remain untouched. God will let me know when to use it and what to use it for. She explained to me that when you figure out what you're meant to do with it, it's going to be something you don't have to work as hard for. I've been through hell and back with being an entrepreneur, she was telling me not to overwork myself when I don't have to, it'll only make it harder on me.

One night I had a weird dream. When I awoke, I told my husband I wanted to open a Wedding Chapel in the building. He was hesitant on the idea because we don't really hear about people getting married too much these days. He didn't want to put money into something that wouldn't earn it back. I knew this was something I was supposed to do. In my heart I knew those buildings were originally meant to be for Ballrooms and Wedding Chapels, and that's what I wanted. I started to work on the idea, I got denied for the loan twice. But the favor that's on my life, God turned that around.

One Sunday when I was leaving church after a service, a young man who attended as well came to me. He asked what I planned to do with the empty building.

I told him how I was still paying taxes on it and was denied a loan twice now. All he told me was, "A friend of mine owes me a favor, I'd like to pass that favor onto you." Three months later I received an approval to get my whole building remodeled. His favor is the reason that I am where I am today. I learned so much through that process, you can't give up when you know God spoke to you. You never know how your blessing is coming. I thank God for always using vessels to push his children to become overcomers.

I didn't realize it at the time, but my grand opening was on the anniversary of my mom passing. The ballroom has been open for 7 years. This project was one of my proudest moments. I did it all from truly listening to God, remembering advice from my mom, getting so many referrals from my husband and working so hard from the muscle.

When you keep trying and believe in yourself no matter what it looks like, you'll go far. I walk by faith, I take risks, and because of that this world is in my favor.

These next three chapters are connected by blood. You'll see the different tragedies experienced throughout these three generations. Their journey in breaking generational curses was a long one, but they all made it.

Family Secrets

I grew up in a small southern town in Virginia until I was 14 years old, we moved to a town near Wilmington, Delaware. High school up North was a culture shock. Coming from a small country town, my new town seemed like a big city to me.

The city of Wilmington was terrifying. I went to school with a lot of people from the city, but I stayed away. Being a country girl, just the stories alone made me not even want to visit. I was this little sheltered girl who wasn't able to go out much back in my small town. I was terrified of pretty much everything. Now that I look back, I realize that all the trauma that I had been through before had turned me into a very fearful, withdrawn person. I was a quiet teenager. In a room full of people, you wouldn't immediately notice me. I avoided conversation, I wanted to be left alone. I was in a lot of emotional turmoil at the time. My family had recently broken up and in my mind, it was all my fault.

I wished I hadn't told my secret. For a while, I blamed myself that my father touched me in inappropriate ways. I should have been relieved that my mother got me out of that situation, but in the back of my mind I felt like she blamed me for the split of our family.

She didn't say she blamed me, I just felt like she did. I could see the pain in her face, and as a young girl, I blamed myself for her pain.

I was so hurt and guilty. In my head, it was my fault we had to leave the only home we had known. I never wanted men to see me like my daddy saw me, so I tried to be as quiet as possible. If I were quiet enough, then maybe no one would see me. I wanted to try my best to be pretty much invisible.

I had a normal childhood up until around twelve. I come from a two-family household. My father had a good job, my mother was a stay-at-home mom. Once she had started working, the abuse started. We had always been in a toxic household.

My dad was mentally abusive towards my mom. With us children, he didn't really pay us any mind. Until he started to pay attention to me, but this wasn't the kind of attention I wanted. I used to watch tv shows and wished my dad would interact with us the way tv dads interacted with their children.

I wished he would tell us how much he loved us, hug us, and tell us how proud he was of us. I even wished he'd tell my mother how much he loved her, compliment her, make her feel like a wife with a husband who cherished her, but he didn't. He was too consumed in his own life to care.

Every evil thing a man could say to a woman, he said to her. My dad used my mom as his verbal and physical punching bag. I prayed that one day things would get better, nothing changed for the best. At 13, he started to pay a lot of attention to me, and not in a safe way. I was now being abused, but not like my mom.

He wasn't talking down to me or being violent to me like he was to her. He was being overly nice, and it was confusing. I lived in a really strict household where we weren't able to do things unless it was with our family or church. Once the abuse started, my dad started to give me more freedom. Allowing me to go to school games, hang out with my friends, even give me spending money.

I loved the freedom, but I hated my dad touching my body parts. I'd cry, and beg him to stop, he wouldn't. I was trying to figure out what I had done to make my daddy want to touch me in a sexual way. Convincing myself no one would believe me; I kept it all in. I became angry, so I started to act out. I'd skip school and hang around the wrong people.

My best friend ended up telling her own mother the truth. She kept the secret for a month. She was trying to protect me. The abuse became a normal routine, and it was turning me into a different person. My mother started to think I was acting out for some boy. I remember the time I was caught skipping school.

That day changed everything. I remember it like it was yesterday. My mom answered the phone after picking me up. After listening to the conversation, I quickly realized it was my best friend's mom she was talking to. I couldn't make out what they were talking about, but I remembered being nervous. I had been in enough trouble for skipping school.

They talked for about a half hour. When my mother got off the phone, she pulled me to the side and told me she needed to talk to me. Her expression and body language were different than anything I ever saw. She asked me if I was being abused while she was at work, and I froze. I didn't want to say yes, and I didn't know how to say no.

I was so ashamed. It was hard for me to get the words, but I could tell from the look in my mother's eyes I needed to tell her. At that moment I felt something I hadn't felt since my dad started touching me. I felt safe. Before I knew it, we were out of the home and relocated to a place where we didn't know anyone.

I felt guilty for breaking the family up, I became a different person. I didn't know at that time, but my life would forever change and emotionally I would never be the same.

My dad was allowed to move back in with us a few years later. Although he never abused me again, or from my knowledge any of my siblings, he didn't change much. He fought the same demons. A few years after he rejoined our home, he was arrested for molesting a girl in the neighborhood. The shame that hung over our family was unbearable, but instead of talking about it or getting any type of counseling, we just went on with our lives. The problem was how the trauma would affect us all in our adult life.

Even though they've been bonded by blood their whole lives, the life she lived was completely different than her older sister's. Both deeply affected by the trauma that occurred from their childhoods. You just finished a heartbreaking story, now you're stepping into Sandy's point of view. If you think it's going to be similar to the previous story you're deeply mistaken. Their struggles were nowhere near the same, but still equally effective.

I suffered alone

Sandy

I was raised in a religious household. We were in a Pentecostal church, we pretty much lived there. We couldn't do things normal children would do. We weren't allowed to play with our friends or go to events at school or after church. We were at the church at least four times a week, sometimes more than that, especially in the summertime. Our mother was really strict.

We didn't come from a very loving home; I never saw my father hug or kiss my mother. I never really saw him show her any affection. They were cold to each other. My dad was actually mean towards my mom. He said and did things that could break any woman. I guess my parents were the reason I chose the type of men I did.

We never really did anything as a family except go to church. We never went on vacations, we just lived to exist. I was a completely withdrawn child. I never felt connected to anyone. As an adult, my childhood affected me tremendously.

I gravitated to the same type of situations I grew up in. Women will always find men who resemble their fathers in some way. I just always felt like I'd rather have some love than no love. My past affected how I chose my spouses. My first ex-husband used me as a punching bag any chance he got.

My second husband was really mentally abusive. I don't believe I was open to loving him the way he needed me to. I had endured so much pain in my first marriage, it changed me completely. I was never the woman to show a lot of emotion. It was just the way I was raised, but my first marriage almost made me numb.

I got pregnant when I was fifteen. I don't think I loved my daughter's father. It was more like I loved the way he made me feel. He was very affectionate; he gave me all the love I felt like I was missing at home. My family was going through so much at the time, but nobody talked about our family issues. We didn't comfort each other or embrace one another, we just kept going. We were pretty much mimicking our mother. At the time I met my daughter's father, I was looking for some type of emotional connection. I thought I was in love at

first, but I wasn't. Getting pregnant wasn't part of
the plan. I was ashamed of myself when I found out.
I felt like I had shamed the family, even though we
were taught to never shame our family. That's why
my mother was so strict in keeping us in church. My
mom wanted us to be respectable, but what we saw
in our home behind closed doors wasn't very
respectable. Still, I felt like I disappointed my
parents, myself, and most of all God. Still, I craved
the affection my child's father gave me.

It was like my emotions were all over the place. I
waited about 4 months to tell my mom. I prayed so
much the entire time I hid it from her. I needed God
to forgive me. I just remembered how depressed I
was.

My dad was being arrested for molesting a young
lady in the neighborhood. I always wondered why
my mom wasn't angrier with my dad. It wasn't his
first time doing something like this. He had done it

to my sister when we were younger. My mom left him for a while, but for some reason he moved back.

My sister may think I didn't know anything about her situation because I was so young. I remember laying in my bed as a little child listening to my sister try to fight our father off. I remember her crying, telling him to get off of her. I was the youngest sister, there was nothing I could do. I remember laying in my bed silently crying for my sister. I will never forget, but I never spoke about it. I wished I had told my mom what he had been doing to her. She was able to get help eventually, years later she forgave him. He never touched me or my other siblings. He chose my sister's best friend, and while all this was going on, I was about to bring a child into the world. I felt guilty because my mom was going through so much, but I wanted to keep my baby. I needed someone who would love me unconditionally.

Eventually I told my mom I was pregnant. She didn't react like I thought she would, she must have been drained. My daughter brought some happiness to the family. She was a beautiful baby. The love I thought I needed from her father couldn't compare to the love I received from her.

The unconditional love I longed for was found in my little baby. For a while life was good for us, but it wasn't long before my baby dad's protectiveness turned into control. Maybe it was always there, maybe I didn't see it because his love was enough at the time. Things had changed, now I was responsible for another little person. He had changed also. The safety I thought I found in him was no longer there. He had his own mental health issues to deal with.

I was sixteen when my daughter was born. Determined to provide for her, I worked and went to school to take care of her. The relationship with my daughter's father had become toxic. He was always threatening to kill himself; I was always trying to make him happy. At 18 I moved into my own apartment and enrolled in my freshman year of college. At this time, I left him and started meeting other guys.

Being single was nice for a while, but by twenty I was married. There were so many red flags to tell me to not marry this man, but the physical attraction was so strong. I should've paid attention to the signs. I didn't know if this man loved me or hated me. Everything that frustrated him in life was taken out on me, physically.

I had been around abusive situations all my life. My very first relationship was abusive, but this was different. I was walking on eggshells every day.

When I met him, I was attracted, because he was so different. He was from the city of Wilmington, and we lived in the suburbs. He was a bad boy, and I was a church girl.

I was going to save him, and we would grow together, was what I thought. Not realizing how damaged he really was and how much he would use everything wrong in his life as an excuse to hit me. It was like it was an emotional release for him to harm me. It wasn't like no one warned me. My sister used to be friends with his ex, she told me he used to beat her really bad.

I don't know why I didn't walk away after that. On top of everything, his ex was the same friend my dad was in jail for molesting. There were so many signs to walk away but I didn't, and I paid for it. Every milestone I should've been happy about, he took away from me by beating on me. He smashed a sandwich in my face, the day before our wedding.

I remember going home, getting in the tub, and crying so hard. Mainly because I no longer wanted to marry him. Something told me to walk away, but I couldn't. All of my family had come from Virginia. Everything was planned. I didn't want my mom to be ashamed or embarrassed, so I married him.

He beat me on the day I arrived home from the hospital after birthing our son. I was beaten until I got tired of dealing with it, that was 8 years later. We bought a house in Smyrna; something was telling me to leave him, but I let him come. I wanted to save my marriage. We had a child together and he was a good stepfather to my daughter.

She was two when we got together. He treated her like she was his own. I convinced myself to focus on his good qualities. Less than a month later he punched me in the nose while I was driving, and blood was everywhere. I was tired, I was done. From that night the relationship was over.

It wasn't easy. I had a new mortgage of 1900 a month, making 13 an hour. I had to take on a second job to make ends meet. I had two children to take care of on my own. I was so depressed. I was trying so hard to heal.

I thought if I provided for my children, I would be ok. I was just doing what I saw my mother do all my life. Picking up the pieces. I began working all time and on top of that I was in school. Although I was doing it for my children, they were suffering because they never got to see me. I was always working and when I wasn't I was tired.

My children were always at someone else's house. They never really spent time in the house, I was fighting so hard to take care of them. During this time my daughter was molested in a household that I thought was a safe place for her, my sister in law's house. We were close and the children loved her. Her husband, whom I also trusted, sexually violated my oldest daughter.

I don't know how I didn't lose my mind. I had to find the strength to fight for my daughter. I did my best with what little strength I had left. Shortly after, I went into a deep depression.

Later on in life I found out I had breast cancer. I was again alone, fighting a battle by myself, fighting for my life. I listened to my children who were telling me how by working all the time, I affected their lives. The time I needed kind words and hugs, all I received was blame for every mistake I made.

But I made it through. God blessed me with the most loving grandchildren and their love pulls me through. I'm now cancer free. I opened up my second daycare center. I'm working on my mental health and hopefully this project will be the first step of healing my family. We need to learn how to communicate with each other, hopefully we can start.

These days I focus a lot on building my dreams. I'm focusing on family and building stronger relationships with my children. I'm a cancer survivor. During the time I was fighting cancer I never felt more alone and depressed. You'd think I would build a closer relationship with my children at that time, but no. We did have a lot of discussions. I was so focused on making sure they didn't need anything financially, that I forgot to make sure I was physically there for them as well.

Briana, the daughter of Sandy. She is one of the youngest members of our anthology. You know the youngest of the clan is usually the wisest. One of the first things she said when asked to describe her family was, "It's full of women with strong personalities who don't really know each other well. When we finally do get together, we don't talk about anything important." She brought up how she once mentioned bringing the family together at an event and was shut down by her aunt, one of her favorite relatives. She would have thought out of all people her aunt would agree. This was how things were with her mom's side of the family. So many secrets.

Briana

My name is Briana Bowman, I am from Clayton, Delaware. I'm married with two kids, another one on the way. I grew up in a small household with my mother, stepdad and two siblings (a sister and a brother). When my mom and stepdad divorced it was just us. She worked a lot, so we spent a lot of time with other family members. It caused me to grow up really fast. Much faster than I would have liked.

I never knew that going to the altar for prayer would change my life. I just needed to get this heavy burden off my heart. I'd been hiding so many secrets and it was starting to weigh me down. It felt like everything happening to me was my fault. I prayed so hard for my uncle to stop hurting me, touching me.

I almost began to believe he was obsessed with doing these sick things to me. It was easy for him to do it without my aunt knowing, she had multiple sclerosis. She could barely get around, forced to stay in her bedroom most of the day. She was one of my favorite people in this world. Our close bond is the reason I kept the secret for so long. I didn't want to lose her.

At the time I was young and naive. Now that I'm older, I believe she knew, or at least had a feeling of what her husband was doing to me. I used to enjoy summers with my aunt, we had a lot of freedom. Of course, I hadn't realized that the type of freedom we were receiving wasn't meant for underaged children. My uncle would give us wine coolers, encouraging us to get drunk. Then we'd have a movie night where the film was nothing but pornos.

My aunt watched with us sometimes too. It's why I question how oblivious she truly was to the situation. The day I went to the altar to ask for prayer about my uncle I felt like I had no other choice. He was becoming more aggressive with me. I would walk in on him doing things like sniffing my underwear.

He'd start to have his son to perform sexual acts on me or vice versa. One of his other sons admitted to me that he didn't like it either. As the touching and groping became more frequent and forceful, I became afraid of him. I approached the altar, when asked what I needed prayer for, I didn't hesitate to answer. I told her my uncle touches children. She asked if he'd touch me. Without thinking, I answered truthfully. Most would think telling makes things better, it only turned my life upside down more.

My mom wasn't one of those parents who dismissed the situation. She focused on locking him behind bars, but what I wanted at the time was love. I needed my mom to embrace me and to tell me it would all be okay. I held resentment towards my mom for years because she couldn't give me what I needed at that time. It wasn't until recently that I realized it wasn't that she wasn't being supportive, we had two different love languages. I wanted to be embraced and comforted. She wasn't used to it. Since then, my love language has changed. Now I can be kind of standoffish.

My childhood trauma has definitely affected my adult life. I'm not good at intimacy, even when it comes to my husband. He has been so patient and good to me. Maybe even too nice. It caused me to be abusive to him, sometimes even physically.

He never was argumentative. I turned him into a different person, forcing him to have to defend himself against me when all he wanted to do is love me. I know I have to deal with all my pinned-up anger, which is why I decided to tell my story.

I grew up in a toxic household where my stepdad beat my mom. He would throw her down the steps, punch her in her face, just pretty much hit on her for no reason, other than the fact that he could. Anytime he was angry or frustrated he would always take it out on her. I was used to seeing my mom cry.

I was used to the screaming, yelling, or just walking on eggshells so she wouldn't set him off. Sometimes they were happy, but even then, I was always preparing myself for when they would get into a fight. Even when he was hugging her, I would be scared that he would just get mad and hit her. You just never know when their happy moment would turn into a fight. Although my stepfather was so abusive to my mom, he never hit me.

He treated me like I was his daughter. I never felt any different from my siblings until I got older. My mom had a different bond with my younger siblings which made me extremely jealous of them growing up. I wasn't the best big sister. I was mean to both of my siblings growing up. Even now we aren't close, even though I would like to be. I just feel like I suffer from so much trauma that it's hard for me to have healthy relationships. Even with the people, who I should be the closest to. I have many unresolved issues. It's hard for me to show emotion other than anger.

My goal for being part of this anthology is to heal and to reach other young women like myself who have been violated as children. I want to create a safe spot for children who suffer any type of trauma.

If they are able to heal, then maybe they won't allow their adult lives to be affected by all the trauma of their childhood.

My first book will be released in August. "Let God Heal What You Concealed." This book is just the beginning of me using my story to help others heal. Hopefully, I can do more healing through this process as well.

Dr. Gabrielle never wanted to go through trials and tribulations as a child. Coming from a background with no money, she had to get a job at an early age. Working and studying paid off for her. Now that she is a multi-business entrepreneur, her story teaches a lesson that hard work and financial literacy can change your life.

Hard Work and Financial Literacy

Dr. Gabrielle

My name is Dr. Gabrielle. I was born and raised in Saint Louis, Missouri. In 2015, For the last 7 years, I have worked as a pharmacist. I went into the Saint Louis College of Pharmacy to receive my qualifications to become Director of pharmacy for a small pharmaceutical company.

I really was into finance and numbers, but when I made the design of what I wanted to do with my life I really wanted to help people.

After graduating college, I finally experienced what it was like to have financial stability. Growing up, money was never a topic that was discussed in the household. My mom was a single mother of three and at the time the only thing I knew and understood about money was that it was in short supply. After graduating, I was making a good salary, living well below my means and able to afford the things in life that I used to consider a luxury. I didn't want to repeat the cycle of financial burden. I decided to educate myself and find a financial advisor to teach me the best ways to save and invest my income. I started studying the traditional personal finance books and found an amazing advisor who told me all the right things to invest in - 401k, Life Insurance, Roth IRA.

However, it didn't take long before I realized that the only financial advice being presented, through books and advisors, involved me working until I was sixty-seven ½. Even with a good paying career, I was told that to secure my financial future I would have to work for years with the hopes I didn't outlive my retirement savings. In addition to that, I still didn't have a good understanding of the principles involving money or investing.

Then one day I read the book *Rich Dad Poor Dad*. This book completely changed my perspective on what it meant to build wealth and become financially independent. Since that day, I committed to increasing my financial literacy and learning about investing. I knew I did not want to work until I was almost seventy and I did not want to have to guess what age I would die to sustain my money through retirement. What I wanted was to find a way to build and sustain generational wealth and create opportunities for myself and my family. *Rich Dad Poor Dad* helped me develop understanding of how money worked, how investing worked and how important it was to be financially literate.

In my quest to build wealth, I started to study real estate. At that time, I saw it as a means to an end. I had no idea just how passionate I would become on the topic of real estate Investing. But over the years, I would buy every real estate book, listen to every podcast, and take down hundreds of pages of notes before I finally got the courage to buy my first property in 2019. That has since led to the purchase of several other real estate investments.

Growing up, information on financial literacy was not as readily accessible as it is today, especially in the black community. As a result of this and several other factors, many of our parents and our parents' parents weren't able to take advantage of the many ways there are to build wealth in this country. One of those ways is through real estate and home ownership. Real estate is an important factor in bridging the wealth gap in our community. In my time as an investor, I have learned about the financial benefits and the ways real estate builds generational wealth for individuals and families. However, one thing I continuously notice is that women of color are not always represented in this market.

As a result, I created a community as an educational platform directed at women and specifically women of color. My goal is to provide information on ways for women to invest their money, educate them on how to buy their first real estate property and also how to utilize the resources they have to build their financial futures. I am someone who decided to take control of her finances to increase my understanding of how to build wealth and financial freedom and I am hoping to do the same for others.

I heard a saying that the ones who go out their way to make you the happiest are almost always the same ones who suffer through pain. After interviewing Tynee, I realized not only is it true, but a lot of times it starts at a very young age. Tynee knew early on, if you make people laugh then they wouldn't laugh at you. What started out as a means for survival, ended up being a career.

Laugh My Pain Away

Tynee

Most people know me as Tynee Laughter. Comedy has always been my biggest defense mechanism. Ever since I was a little girl, I always made people laugh. I wasn't the best-looking child. I was made fun of for everything. I needed to leave to make people laugh with me, so they'd forget to laugh at me.

Growing up for me was bitter. In the beginning we had a two-parent home. All of a sudden, my father was no longer in the picture. My mother moved us to eastside and lived as a single parent for a little bit. Eventually she got in another relationship with a man who later became our step daddy. It was hard because I was a daddy's girl. To this day, I have no idea why they divorced.

I do remember the last argument they had. I'm not sure what it was about, but I do remember how scary it was this time. It didn't take me too long to figure out he wasn't coming back. I tried to keep the thought away. It was over once I started seeing other men come around.

I was the only child that my parents shared together. I took the split up harder than my siblings. My dad was a father figure to my two older siblings as well. I'm sure they were sad about the change as well. Just not as affected as me.

When I was around 6 or 7 my mom suffered from an addiction. During that time, I had no idea where the sudden change in her behavior stemmed from. She already used to drink when she was with my father. They'd argue every now and then, but I never knew what about. I'm not even sure whether she had been on drugs while he was still in the picture as well.

After a while, my mom got into another relationship. Since he wasn't my dad, I didn't take a liking to him right away. As I got older, he grew on me. Now he's like another dad. My mom and him are still together.

Becoming Tynee The comedian

During my middle school years, I was basically a tomboy. It was hard keeping friends because my family had moved around a lot. It was worse trying to make friends. The other girls in my school were into fashion and makeup, I was not. I was obsessed with comedy jams, so I used to sneak and watch it. Watching the show pretty much taught me how to crack jokes on the people who teased me. The others would make fun of my looks a lot. I wasn't the typical pretty, athletic girl and they'd never let me forget it. Once I started clapping back with funny jokes, it seemed like things started to get better for me. I always made them laugh.

I became a comedian early on without even realizing. My aunt was real spiritual, she would always tell me that comedy was my calling. I would study comedy shows. It was really all I wanted to watch. The more I watched, the funnier I became. Overtime, my confidence grew a little.

In high school I was semi popular, I didn't have a lot of friends, just a small group. Everyone still knew I was considered the class clown. They would laugh at all my jokes. I did have two good friends who were sisters. I met them years before when my parents split up.

We've been friends for a long time. I even stayed at their house for a while during my last year of high school. They had a brother who I dated for a short while too. Those two sisters were my support system throughout the school year. I don't know how I would've made it without them.

I remember my first gig like it was yesterday. The opportunity was in Delaware, I didn't reside there at the time. I lived in North Carolina. Someone close to me had passed away, I just couldn't miss her funeral. She was someone really special to me. When I got to my hometown my mom was throwing a barbecue. I'm doing what I normally do, saying shit that'll make everyone laugh. A friend of my mom's pulled me to the side and asked me to open for his band at their next gig. He knew I wasn't really a comedian. He believed I could do it. Having real confidence is a new feeling to me. False confidence is what got me through school. I didn't become confident until I left a very toxic relationship. This relationship had taken so much out of me that I needed to go to therapy. A lot of

black people don't believe in therapy, but it's
changed my life.

I never thought I'd get to the point in my life where
the opinions of others didn't matter. Now I'm
building, getting on stage, traveling, and making
people laugh. It's not easy and sometimes I get
discouraged but it makes me happy. Everything I've
been through has gotten me to this moment. This
month I will grace multiple dissimilar stages and
continue to grow until I am on your tv screen with
my own segment.

Being a caretaker can be hard for anybody. When your child is fighting for her life, it's a whole different battle. Agatha had to battle the healthcare system just to make sure her daughter had every opportunity possible. During that battle she learned of the pressure and drama that came with raising a sick child in a weak family foundation.

Agatha

My name is Agatha Thomas, and I was born in Brooklyn, New York. Now I live in Delaware. Before I moved to Delaware I lived in Atlanta with my sister and her husband. They moved there when they came up with a business idea they wanted to pursue. They were tired of New York and wanted a fresh start.

Atlanta was a good place for them to start the new business. They asked me to come and help them with the children. I had just finished my 2 years in business school and pursued my paralegal degree. I knew relocating could be an amazing opportunity for me but at the time I didn't really want to go. New York was the only place I had known.

It was a hard decision for me to make. After thinking about it, I finally agreed. My sister convinced me it would be a good fresh start. Life was too short to just stay in one place all your life. When I got to Atlanta, I loved it.

There was always something to do. I was at every event. Partying, drinking, traveling with my new friends going back and forth to Florida. I didn't have any children at that time. I was just doing me, having an enjoyable time.

When I first moved there, I wasn't sure how long my stay would be. I didn't necessarily have any goals yet, so I just hung out a lot. I was social, I made friends pretty easily. Instead of driving, my friends would take me around since it wasn't guaranteed that I'd move there permanently. I didn't want to risk paying on a car that I wouldn't keep. Later, I started working for Bank of America. I then got into doing contract work in Chicago, flying back and forth to Atlanta. As that started to taper away, I decided I wanted more for myself and stopped the partying altogether. I joined church and joined the choir. My church, Victory World, was a big church. People from all walks of life attended. I got saved and adapted to a new type of lifestyle. Some of the members are still my friends today. Atlanta was the highlight of my life. I was exposed to many different things and learned a lot. I stayed there for 13 years. After I had given my life to the lord, I knew it was time to leave Atlanta. It was time to find new growth within myself in a new environment. I was ready to settle down, so I moved to Delaware. Being financially, mentally, and spiritually on top of my game I was more than ready to get into the dating life. Only, it seemed like every man that was on my level came to be extremely controlling.

Men wanted to marry me, but their plan was for me to be a stay-at-home mom. That's not what I wanted. I needed to be able to follow my dreams. I came to the conclusion that I would entertain a man who had some potential. By the time I met my husband I was at a low point in my life.

We were having a lot of problems; my sisters and I were constantly going at it. My mom had five girls and 2 boys. One of my sisters was raised in New York while my other sister was raised in another country. My mom left her there, so she'd be able to get her life together here. I love being around my family but there may have been some resentment from my sisters.

When I first came to Delaware, I was staying with two of my other sisters. While living there it was working out with us three. One night a big fight happened, and I packed my bags. One of my girlfriends from church told me to come stay with her. I rented a room from her for a while then eventually rented out her basement. It wasn't too long before I took on a second job as a property assistant and got an apartment on the property.

I met my husband on a dating app. We met up in New York and we hit it off from there. At one time he wanted me to move back to New York. I considered it, but for whatever reason every time I applied for a job, I wouldn't get it. After I had gotten pregnant with my son, staying in Delaware was a no brainer. I began to receive more opportunities that would help me out. Clearly, I was meant to stay.

Instead of leaving, I told him to move to Delaware. There were a lot of open conversations about the idea. He hadn't known anything about Delaware. He proposed before we could decide what to do with the moving situation. In the end, the deal was we'd go back to New York if he couldn't find peace in Delaware.

We got a bigger apartment in the complex. I moved my mother in with me to help me with the baby. That's when all hell broke loose. Being newly married, having a new baby, and bringing a parent to come live with you on top of that can cause chaos. I hadn't thought it through.

In my mind, I assumed that my mom would be a tremendous help while I went back to work. They just didn't get along, I guess I should've laid down ground rules, but I didn't. We bought a bigger house and at the time I got pregnant. With this baby, I had a miscarriage while visiting my husband's family on vacation.

I walked into the townhouse we were staying in. There was a puddle on the marble floor. At the time I didn't pay attention to it. My husband has tried to engage in a conversation about it, but I assured him I was fine. By the time I woke up the next morning I had already started miscarrying the baby.

While bending over to get a shirt I got dizzy. I needed to sit down; it was starting to feel like I was having some type of discharge. When I went to the bathroom to check, all I saw was blood. I immediately went into the hospital, scared because we were out of the country, and I wasn't used to international hospitals. The baby passed, it wasn't too much of a heartbreak, I wasn't really ready for another child.

Within a month I was pregnant again. I wasn't too happy at the time of finding out, I was sick of being pregnant. I had a lot of goals I wanted to achieve. Once the pregnancy started to advance, I realized my husband didn't show the same happiness he did when I was pregnant with my son after finding out we were having a girl. He wasn't that supportive; he was in denial about it for a while.

Once I had my first sonogram, they found something irregular. I remember sitting in the doctor's office by myself, scared and nervous, waiting for information as to what they saw. I could see one doctor looking and the other doctor calling another. I knew something was wrong. I started talking to God as I waited.

They sent images over to a heart doctor in Nemours Children's Hospital and they sent me on my way to him as well. He told me he saw something in the heart area. I didn't worry too much. Many babies are diagnosed with different things during the pregnancy, it doesn't mean they are born that way. My husband went through the same experience with

his eldest son he had with an ex, he lived, and he
was fine.

We heard what the doctors said, but we didn't claim
it. Still, I kept up on all the doctors' appointments.
The doctor let me know that once the child is born,
they'd have to immediately take him because he
wouldn't be able to breathe. I was just confused as
to how they could see all this on a sonogram. I had a
son, and he was healthy.

I was in denial about the possibility of my daughter
being ill. I didn't understand why her birth would be
any more difficult than my sons. It didn't make
sense to me. My husband was disconnected with this
pregnancy, and it made me angry with him. More so
angry with myself for getting pregnant again.

Once it was time for her to be born there were a lot
of people in the room. My daughter had her own
team. I had good doctors and was set to have a c
section. After they took the baby, I got a call that

she needed a blood transfusion because she was losing multiple blood cells. I gave the approval for the first blood transfusion, two hours later they called for the approval of another blood transfusion, the first one didn't take.

My husband wasn't handling things the way I would have. He was overwhelmed, and my sister, who was also there, didn't really care for my husband. I requested to be discharged early. I couldn't sit another night in the hospital not fully understanding what was going on with my daughter.

Entering the hospital where there were only patients of sick children was depressing. They had my baby secluded in her own room; I wouldn't leave her side. I basically took over and did what I was allowed to do by myself. Being in a children's hospital was nerve racking. I needed to make sure my daughter wasn't assigned any stressed-out doctors or overworked nurses.

I almost never went home. I barely saw my son; we'd talk on the phone. My family started to get worried about me. My husband was really distant at this time. My mother and I started doing shifts. Growing up, my mom always told me you never leave your loved ones in the hospital. The doctors ended up suggesting I leave anyway. They feared I'd get an infection; I hadn't fully healed from the C section. I was also under too much stress. I wasn't on bedrest like I was supposed to be. My daughter had been more important.

The family came together and really helped me take care of Anna. My husband wasn't too happy around the time. When you have a sick child, it puts a lot of strain on your family. For my family, everything ended in a messy divorce. I fought hard for my daughter.

Stay tuned for the full story about everything that happened within our family and how we overcame all of our obstacles. Being a mother of a child with special needs can change your entire world, but for Anna I will never stop fighting.

This next chapter is something I think most Christians go through at some point. The conversation of how not all church folks is godly is a huge topic in this world. Lovely's journey is about her place within the church and how the members around her would only confuse her. You'll see how the drama of the church only pushed her farther away. It wasn't easy for her, especially coming from a strict household.

I Always Had Questions

Lovely

My name is Lovely Thornton and I'm originally from Antonio Texas. For the past 3 years I've been living in Philadelphia, Pennsylvania. I got to the point that I needed and desired a change. The last few years were about reconditioning. I needed to unlearn what I grew up with. As I continued to relearn and grow, I almost started to feel like a different person. Moving out of my environment was the first step towards growth for me. I loved Philly, but I could never live there forever. It just seemed like the more I tried to move, the harder it was to get the means to do it.

All doors were being slammed in my face. I couldn't transfer the job I worked with at the time. I was trying to get to Houston Texas. Instead, I was forced to stay in Philadelphia. Moving out was a hard process, and there was no point in leaving if I had no job to fall back on. It was out of my control.

As a child I was raised as a Christian. My mom and dad were never married but they were both heavy in church. They were supposed to get married when my mother was pregnant with me, but my father changed his mind. They weren't in love, and my father didn't want to make a commitment he wasn't true to. I understood that.

We moved around a lot when I was a child. Everywhere we went was of Christian faith. Most of my time was spent in the church. My parents made sure I participated in all of the church activities. There wasn't a church event that I didn't attend.

I was raised by two parents who only knew church. My upbringing was extremely strict and sheltered for that reason. It was hard to adapt to my environment because we'd move around a lot. That means I went to countless different schools over the school years. So, I was reserved and quiet.

In the church I came across a lot of different personalities. By that, I mean everyone was two faced. It'd confuse me to watch the adults in my life just constantly lie. Especially when I was told to always tell the truth. Watching them trash talk people they'd claim to care about never sat right with me, even as a child.

I was a very observant child. The amount of gossiping, putting others down, spreading rumors, etc. It made me question everything. Christians weren't supposed to behave like this. They took pride in it too. I was a naturally curious child; I didn't understand how it was normal. If you're supposed to leave everything unlike God outside the church, then why did they do these things?

When I started getting older, I became curious like I was as a younger child. It bothered me that no one would answer my questions. Any time my question sounded like I was wavering in my belief, I'd be shut down. I had to do my own research. When I did, I put my own feelings and knowledge about church to the side so that I'd be looking with an open mind.

What I came up with is that we're not here just by chance. There are too many unexplainable things that happen in this world for a higher power to be false. It would be ignorant to act naive. I've seen a lot of things happen that wouldn't make sense. I have a lot of unanswered questions; I would say now I am much more spiritual than religious.

As a teenager I was rebellious in a sneaky way. I was really into the internet and tv. Music and books were the gateway into a different world. I didn't smoke until I was 19-20. I skipped school a few times with my friends, it wasn't too crazy. but growing up in such a strict religious environment those things would be considered extreme.

It was a point where no matter what I'd do, it ended in me being yelled at, or beat. By that point, I just wanted to live my life and deal with the consequences later. I knew not to go too far to the point where I'd be kicked out. I'd try to navigate. Since I was older, I recognized more negative things within the church. Too much was going on behind the scenes. Fornication, abortions, publicly shaming women just to accept them back into the church once they start becoming active within the ministry, it was the most unholy place to be. No one ever addressed how messed up it was. They only kept going like it was normal.

I was a survivor. My parents weren't the type to just randomly beat on me. It was more like their faith was rooted in them so deep that any time they felt I was denouncing our religion, they'd be quick to put their hands on me instead of taking the opportunity to teach me. They were the type to shun whoever brought shame to their religion. So as a teenager, there were a lot of different parts of me I had to keep a lot of things separate.

I knew I was queer since an early age. My sexuality was always a strange subject. The way I found out who I truly was just so happened to be some of the darkest days for me. When you are molested or raped at an early age it can cause you to be confused with your sexuality. My earliest memory of being molested is 4 years old.

I was playing hide and seek with my aunt, and she touched me in ways she had no business touching me. At the moment I didn't know what was going on, I just knew that she liked me. Even at an early age, being liked was important. Later it happened with my ex-stepbrother, who was French kissing me and other stuff when I was 6. The two other times it happened was with girls. One was the pastor's daughter, and the other one was my mom's friend's daughter.

Since I was young, the only thing I could register was the fact that they showed a liking to me. It didn't feel like I was being violated at the time. Once I realized how wrong it was, I felt ashamed. I was so desperate to feel some type of attention that I was unknowingly okay with the wrong type. After that I refused to engage in anything sexual. The very idea of sex was automatically demonized.

Everything I felt was wrong. I felt attracted to both boys and girls. It wasn't about what they looked like; it was about the bond I had with them. When my parents realized I wasn't straight, and I had a desire to experience intimacy it was a problem. It was a shock for them, and it turned my high school years into prison years. Only allowed to do things with my church friend.

Another thing that made my parents very upset was when I told them I no longer wanted to go to church. I waited to graduate before breaking the news. Both of my parents still have a huge problem with it. I had to explain, I'm not saying there is no God. That just wasn't the way I wanted to live my life. I didn't need a middleman to connect with God.

Interviewing Mercedes took me through different emotions. Her story shows how she had no other choice but to show up. Mercedes is from the Dominican Republic. Most didn't consider themselves black, I wasn't sure if she'd want to participate in this book. Her response shocked me, she told me the ones who denounce their blackness must be ignorant of their heritage, ancestors, or descendants of Spaniards and Haitians. There are all types of people in the Dominican Republic, she identified as an afro Latina. After learning new history lessons from Mercedes, I knew she was perfect for this project. I just didn't realize how perfect until listening to her story.

Mercedes

My name is Mercedes DeGroot, I'm from New Jersey. For the past 8 months I've been living in Delaware. The cost of living is much less expensive here, and there's no taxes. My husband and I are both retired. I told my husband that I wanted to focus on me once we moved. I deserved to make things about me.

I was born in the Dominican Republic. When I was around the age of two, we moved to the United States. We lived in Florida and stayed there for the majority of my childhood years. In 1973, we moved to New Jersey. It was a struggle for me.

Both of my parents only spoke Spanish. It's all we had known. I remember how hard I struggled in 4th and 5th grade. The difficulty in learning to speak English caused me to believe I was less than the other children. My self-esteem was crippling.

I attended a white school. Making friends wasn't easy. Food was thrown at me, they nicknamed me 'Spic.' The treatment I received was similar to the nerds you'd see being bullied in movies. I never stood up for myself.

I'd hide away and cry. As an adult, I've only recently started becoming more comfortable in defending myself. It was hard being social as a child. Sparking up a conversation seemed to be the hardest thing for me. Being around people was never something I particularly enjoyed. Even in college I remained the same. The idea of engaging in conversations with new people scared me.

Back in 1998 I was diagnosed with a heart murmur and a leaky heart valve. The symptoms started while I was in high school. First it was the joint pain, then skin rashes, I was constantly sick with fevers and headaches. The doctors started running all sorts of tests. It wasn't until 2015 when they diagnosed me with lupus, fibromyalgia, Strogen, and arthritis.

I was prescribed strong pain medication due to the joint pain and because it was extremely hard to focus. I missed out on many workdays. My boss helped me get settled into working at home. With the position I had, I was able to work remotely.

I tried to continue working as long as I could, but it had gotten to the point where it was too tiring. I had no other choice but to start preparing for retirement. It was hard as a wife and a mother, but I was lucky. I knew women whose husbands left them when they're sick because of the pressure.

My husband was always supportive. There were times when I'd become insecure and think he'd leave me one day. I felt guilty for being too sick to attend certain events. He was taking care of me and the kids. I didn't want him to become one day overwhelmed enough to just pack up and go.

The illness affected my children deeply. At young ages they were forced to watch me go in and out of hospitals. I missed out on dance recitals and sports games. My son would cry a lot. He hated that I was in pain. I always encouraged him to be strong.

These last 4 years have been the hardest. I tried two dozen different medications and infusions. Even today I'm still switching between new ones. I now help raise awareness in my community about lupus. I believe my passion and commitment to the cause helped me find my purpose.

In 2017 I started becoming more involved with lupus organizations. Helping people with situations similar to mine made me feel more empowered. I was privileged enough to attend the 15th annual advocate for lupus research day. I've gained another family in those who are also affected with lupus. Life is changing for me. My goal is to learn more about holistic medications. I want to get out of my comfort zone and network with people. I have a clean start now that I've moved to Delaware. I don't want my illness to hold me back anymore. I just want to live a fulfilled life.

Bobby's journey is like no other. The obstacles she was forced to overcome are shocking. You would have never known of all the pain she experienced from one look. Being taken in by her grandmother at an early age was the best thing for her. She may not have always realized it but being away from her mother was a blessing in disguise. Take a glimpse through the life of Bobby and understand her story. It's a rocky one.

Bobbi

My name is Bobbi Dunbar. I'm originally from Saint Gabriel, Louisiana. For the last 4 years I've been in Humble, Texas. It's right outside of Houston, Texas. Moving to Texas wasn't originally my plan. In 2014, I suffered a bad car accident. Rehab was better for me in Texas versus my hometown.

As a child I was pretty quiet. I was the sixth child out of 9. Out of all of them, it felt like I got the least attention. My grandmother raised me. I spent most of my time in church with her.

We went the majority of the week. I loved it when I was younger but as I got older, I started to rebel. Being in the church wasn't what I longed for. It's what I had to do as long as I lived in my grandmother's house. Once I finally turned 19, I moved out on my own and stopped going.

As I got older my personality changed. I was no longer that reserved church girl. I was good with my words; I had a gift to gab. I made people laugh, but I was a loner. Trusting people didn't come naturally. Therefore, I didn't really hang out with a lot of people. I'd go out to parties, but as far as getting close enough to be friends with someone, I wouldn't dare.

I was abandoned with a 10-month-old son when I was 16. My baby dad left me to marry my best friend. It taught me to always keep my guard up. I no longer trusted people, especially females. I kept all my friendships at a safe distance.

My mother and I didn't have a bond. I shared the same fate with my siblings. I've always hated that she didn't interact with me. We lived near each other, but my grandmother barely wanted me to visit. My siblings that lived with my grandmother were raised differently than the siblings that lived with my mom.

Our houses were all built within each other, it was like three houses in one. My mother lived with three of my siblings in the first house. My grandfather built it for my grandmother, it was located in the front yard. My grandma and I lived in the back house. The third house was just a few feet away. Now that I'm older, I'm glad I was raised with her. I would be a completely different person if I hadn't. My sisters and I weren't raised the same. My mom's house was a fun house. There was no parental guidance.

The neighborhood children ran in and out of there. They partied a lot and gambled. Boys were always hanging in there. It's why my grandmother basically forbade me to go over. My mother didn't care to see me, so it didn't bother her.

The only time I got to hang with my other siblings was when my grandmother did their hair. She put a wedge between us whenever they were there. She'd speak of them as if they were no good because of their lifestyle. It made them resent us; we resented them more over the fact that they got to be with our mom. Sibling rivalry started from toxic adults. We never learned to be close to each other.

My mom had nine children. Her first three boys, two with the same dad. She left them with my grandmother once she got married. After two more children, I came. She had two more after me with my father. Our youngest sister was conceived with someone else.

I wasn't always with my grandmother. We stayed with my mom and dad for years. He was an alcoholic, he'd abuse her. She would run away but she always left us behind. Later he became paranoid about whether I was truly his or not. When he started to beat on me, my grandma stepped in. When he got drunk, he'd take it out on all of us in the house. I remember how he'd push my brother down the stairs or pinch my body all up. We were the two he didn't really care for. I'm grateful for my grandmother taking me in. Later, she took in my baby sister.

I was twenty-six when I got on drugs. All my priorities and dreams ended when I started to smoke crack. My relationship with my mom was better because she'd do drugs with me and my sisters at times. I will never forget the time she passed me a pipe. She'd even try to use me to get drugs from the local drug dealer by hooking up with them.

It never registered how she didn't care about me until she needed me for drugs or money. After a while, my habit became worse. I remember letting local drug dealers use my car in exchange for drugs. I had to chase them around trying to get my car back, or I'd negotiate for extra drugs. This is when I knew I had hit rock bottom.'

It wasn't until my last car accident leaving me disabled that made me realize what I was doing. I had always known God and I knew that I was allowing the devil to stir me from my calling. Eventually, I got clean and learned to better myself. That's when I had made the decision to stay in Texas.

Since the car accident my quality of life has changed. I have to wait for someone to dress, feed, and bathe me. No longer able to walk, I have to rely on a scooter to get me around. Wrapping my head around the idea of having a caregiver bothered me. This past month hasn't been any easier.

I'm not going to end this chapter with inspiration and promises of a better life. As I wrapped up this project, I received some news. This news I received has broken my spirit into pieces. I can't be strong for anyone right now because I feel betrayed by God.

I want to yell and scream at the top of my lungs, to beg God for answers. I survived many heartbreaks, drug addictions, three car accidents, and the deaths of my loved ones. I don't know if I have the strength for my new battle. Usually I'm the prayer warrior, but this time around I have never been angrier with God.

Learn more about my latest battle and how I'm coping in my new book that was released on August 12th, 2022 **"I Didn't Know I was Unbreakable,"** it'll change lives. Make sure to keep my family in your prayers.

Onsujii is a living testimony. The journey she faced was a rough one. Her path was one of addiction. She shares how it affected her and how she made it out. Onsujii is a lucky one, not everyone could survive what she went through. God truly had favor on her and had his arms wrapped around her.

From the Streets To The Stage

Onsujii

My name is Onsujii, I'm from Chicago, Illinois. I now live in Stockbridge, Georgia right outside Atlanta. I've been in the Atlanta area for the past 18 years. I've lived in four different states altogether. When I moved to Atlanta, I was running from demons, but I carried them with me. I was running from a troubled relationship and a worse drug habit. I came to Atlanta to try and start fresh. When I got there, I was clean for a good 6 to 7 months. An instance in another relationship is when things started to go wrong. I ran straight to drugs. It took me 5 years to get clean again, and these 5 years were treacherous.

Those last years of my drug life were the worst. I didn't go to rehab when I decided to get clean. Jail played a huge part in me getting off of drugs. I was sick and tired. I just told myself that I wasn't going to get high anymore and pushed away any thoughts about it.

I was addicted to crack cocaine for 22 years. I lost my children twice. I relapsed after getting them back. The last few years I was out in the streets, broke. Homeless moving from palace to place. It was getting bad.

I wronged a lot of people in the neighborhood. Due to my addiction, I'd get mixed up with the wrong people. I had been in debt with dangerous people. In order to help myself, I'd rob my neighbors without a care in the world. If I needed to hit you in the head with a bottle for drug money, or to pay someone off, I would.

For me, everything started when I was 18 years old. It was 1996, I had just graduated high school. Coming from a childhood full of sexual abuse, neglect, and physical abuse made me struggle to find my identity. I had extremely low self-esteem. It wasn't hard to fall down the wrong road.

I was always a weed smoker in high school. It was the only drug I had ever done. When I dated my coworker, she introduced me to putting cocaine in my weed. It was so good to me. All of my problems were forgotten. I was relaxed, and confident. I wasn't that shell of a person that I had become because of childhood trauma.

Her and I had eventually fallen out. I didn't realize that she was doing more than smoking the drugs in her weed. She was worsening and I didn't like it. So, I had started to buy my own crack to put in my weed. It was hard trusting people, everyone had ulterior motives.

There was one day when I couldn't find any weed for my crack. I had never gotten high on crack with anything other than weed. There was this guy who taught me how to use a pipe. Originally, I was against the idea. I didn't want to be so high that I'd be unaware of what was happening.

I knew I shouldn't, but he convinced me, and I tried it. I continued for two decades. It was an unbelievable feeling. The biggest rush I felt in my life, I could almost compare it to an orgasm. That feeling I was always chasing ruined my life, it wasn't worth the turmoil it would cause me.

By the time I was fully clean, I had been forty. I missed out on my entire adulthood. Some of my time was spent locked up in Clayton County jail then Cobb County. I was serving time for petty crimes, I had warrants. During that jail time I got angry because I wanted to be high.

First, I was angry that life as I knew it was interrupted by jail. As time passed, I became more okay with being sober. I started to author a book called '**The Devil Who Wrote Me A Letter.**' That's what my life felt like. The devil was mad at me for trying to get my life together.

Unbelievably, once I made the decision to get my life in order everything fell in place pretty fast. I didn't realize that my credit was good because I had never lived normally. I got a decent job and made really good money. I became an actor and a comedian. Everything came full circle within a year. My dreams came true fast. I knew I was blessed.

I've been able to share the stage with a lot of talented people like Peirre Edwards. I recently did a set with CoCo Brown of Tyler Perry. I am currently at the trap music museum. I'm a character named

Trap house Trina, a live prop actress. It's a wonderful place. I'm really thankful for the opportunity.

This new season of my life is about growth. I will be doing more acting roles and my stand-up sets. I am thinking about transitioning into podcasting. I know greatness is in store.

Interviewing this young lady almost made me feel like I was looking into a mirror image of my life. She made me feel like everything she was speaking about was some of the same things I experienced. We had very abusive relationships ending with us both behind bars. The good thing is, God had favor and what we thought was the ending, was just the beginning.

Fighting for my life

Kita Young

Behind closed doors is where I show my emotions

I cry if I feel I can't handle it anymore

When I'm joyful I laugh and dance as if I'm loony

When I'm mad, my poetry comes beautifully

My emotions are themselves when I'm alone

But

In front of you I'm not myself

I don't know how to react around others

Nor do I want

Behind Closed Doors by Yenesis Polanco

My name is Kita Young. I was originally raised in Mississippi, and I now live in Aurora, Colorado. Fresh from Mississippi, I moved to Memphis, Tennessee and started my new life there. It's where I made a lot of mistakes in my life. The last incident with my ex-husband landed me in jail facing some major charges. After the charges were lowered and I was free to go, I knew I had to change my life. I told myself I was going to go where no one knew me and that's just what I did.

I saw a lot at a young age. If I didn't have my twin sister by my side to help me process, I truly don't know where I'd be. The only person that talked calmly to us and didn't raise her voice was my Madia. She was the only calm person I ever had in my life. Everyone else was always so angry all the time.

Everyone yelled, no one held civilized conversations with each other. Chaos was normal in my life.

Growing up I was an angry child. I didn't know where the anger stemmed from until I was way older.

I grew up with my father and his mother Madia. My dad had a girlfriend, but we never called her our mom, my grandmother was our mother figure. I'm biracial. My dad was white, while my mom was black.

I had no idea what she even looked like for a while. Imagine how devastated we were to find out our dad was going to jail, and we'd be going to live with her. We didn't even know her. Dad's mother was who we considered a mom. As soon as we moved there our childhood literally ended.

That's when the anger began. All she did was put a roof over our heads and fed us. Basically, what she needed to do to avoid neglect charges. We nurtured ourselves. All four of us.

My mother had two other children already living with her. We were 5 years apart from both of them, there was one older than us, and the other was younger. It was us against them for a while. There was a lot of tension amongst us at first.

It wasn't until an altercation between my birth mother and oldest sister that we all came to the conclusion that we need to stick together. Our mom was unstable, instead of arguing and fighting amongst each other, we needed to protect one another. None of us are sure why she was so cold. I don't know what her battles were. I never found out.

At the time I felt like there was a lot of hatred towards all of her children. I remember her calling my twin and I all kinds of racial slurs. As a child I really didn't understand. I would like to think that this lady is supposed to be our mom. I know she didn't raise us, but we were her children. What did

we do to her? It wasn't until I was in my twenties
when I discovered why she was the way she was.
I wasn't able to call my dad because he was
incarcerated, and my grandmother was too old to
raise us. My sister and I had become inseparable.
We were almost joined at the hip. We were each
other's security blanket. We were stuck with her; it
was a nightmare we had to adapt to.

Our oldest sister was given the responsibility of
doing our hair. She had already been doing our
younger sisters. My mom expected her to make sure
our hair was done.
Our hair was harder to manage, we had frizzy and
thick textured hair. We'd often get teased about it in
school.
I don't think my mother wanted us to be close. I
remember her walking in the house and seeing my
older sister do my twin's hair on the front porch.

Out of nowhere she started picking a fight. She went into the house then came out and just pushed my oldest sister off the porch for no reason. My big sister got back up and shoved my mom back. Then they fought like they were strangers in the street. Back then the hairbrushes were those wooden hard brushes. My mom picked up the brush and hit my sister in the eye with it. She then grabbed a medal pole with barbed wire wrapped around it and hit my sister in her back two times. My sister was later hospitalized. It was literally us against our mother after that.

Eventually we were removed from the house when we were fifteen. My mother's sister had taken us in, she was no better. She was abusive and, in the streets, selling drugs. She flat out told us to fend for ourselves. My oldest sister tried hard to help us out, but her little McDonald's check wasn't enough.

My aunt would put a lock on her refrigerator so we wouldn't sneak food. One day I was so hungry that I asked her if I could sell some of her weed for food. Surprisingly, she agreed. We eventually turned to selling drugs just so we could eat and have clothes. I sold drugs at my school to make good money.

A lot of guys in the hood would act like they wanted to help us. Eventually they'd try to force themselves on us or other inappropriate things. There was one guy who had been new to town. He was at least 5 years older than me, I instantly connected with him. He treated me so well.
Now that I look back, he was really grooming us for a life of crime. He had me selling drugs and robbing. He'd tell me that my body was better than the strippers we hung around, and that I could be making so much more than them. It was because of him I moved to Memphis. My twin and I were

making so much money that we decided we needed to get our own place. Since we were still too young, my older sister rented the house and we all moved in together.

Later, he was killed in front of me three days after his birthday. I took it awfully hard because he had been the person that helped me have a somewhat stable life. Without my father in my life during my crucial teenage years, he had become the closest thing I had to a male protector. He was the only male guidance on how a female should be treated. Although, him letting me have my way all the time only worsened my "it's my way or the highway" mentality.

Well, that's what I thought at the time. Now that I'm older I know he was just using us to make money. My life began to change after he died, he and my bonus dad had already perfected my drug selling. My crime life increased drastically after losing him.

I eventually moved past it and decided to better myself.

I was going to school, getting my life together. I met this guy who later became my husband. He was different from the type of guys I normally dated. He sold drugs but wasn't really a street guy. At first the relationship was everything I wanted.

We'd get into conflicts a lot after we had gotten married. I would lash out and hit on him during intense arguments. It was a year before he started hitting me back. He began calling the police on me to press charges. Only to drop them right before we go to trial, unless the prosecutor dropped them once they'd realize he bailed me out. One night he went far enough to wake me up out of my sleep with a gun to my head.

Everything about the relationship was toxic. With my ex I think it became something that he liked. He got off on fighting just to make up. I planned to leave, when he found out, that night changed my life. We fought from the back of the house, all the way to the front. Nobody could break us up. Not even after he had picked up a metal chair and hit me with it.

His mom was there, along with my sister and my son. They couldn't stop us. I believe he wanted to kill me. He was hitting me with a chair. Next thing I knew, I was picking up a gun that he must've dropped. We were both scrambling for it, I reached it first. Without another thought, I closed my eyes and pulled the trigger. For a moment, I thought I had died. Years later I still can't remember much of what happened that day. I just know I woke up in a hospital bed then taken to a jail cell because I had shot the man, I once loved for not letting me leave him in peace.

You can read more about the story in my book **"Behind Closed Doors"** now available on Amazon.

This story digs deep into how the trauma of your childhood can affect you as an adult. What I love the most about Bridgett's story is after everything she's been through; she has dedicated her life to helping other people and that God gave her a perfect partner to help her do it. The beginning of the story is heartbreaking, but the amazing woman Bridgett has become after all the trauma she's dealt with is breathtaking.

Unwanted Attention

Bridgett

My name is Bridgett, I'm from New Haven, Connecticut. I've lived in Connecticut since I was 4 years old. I was born in Daytona Beach, Florida to a 16-year-old mother. My first memory of what my family looked like was grandparents, an older brother, and my mom. We were a tight knit family. When I was 2 my mother married my stepdad. They later left for Connecticut and kept us with my grandparents until they were settled. We were reunited with my parents 2 years later when my dad left the service and found a good factory job. My mom was still incredibly young and a stay-at-home mom. I remember catching the train with my grandmother to go meet her. She had me dressed up in a beautiful yellow dress that day.

I remember a beautiful pregnant woman approaching us and my grandmother asking me if I knew who she was. It was my mom. I remember my mom hugging and kissing me and I felt so loved and happy. It's not that I lacked love, my grandparents took loving care of us. Being reunited with my mother was just a feeling I would never forget.

My mom was always the parent that showed her children a lot of love and affection. She must've gotten that quality from my grandmother because they both made us feel loved. When my mom left us with our grandmother it wasn't dramatic. We were okay because my grandmother had always been present in our life. At that moment with my mom, I didn't only feel loved by her, I felt loved by my whole family.

It was a special moment that I remember so clearly from when I was only 4 years old. Knowing that the lady who birthed me loved me as much as I love her was priceless. It was such an amazing feeling. I was happy and excited to be in my new home. My grandmother went home which may have made us a little sad, however she moved to Connecticut a few months later.

Most people wouldn't believe it now, but I was shy as a child. I always knew I had a purpose in life. A lot of things happened when I was young. It's almost like I wasn't supposed to be here. I survived a lot of things that could have been tragic.

At almost 2 years old, I crossed the street and was seconds away from being hit by a big Mack truck. When I was 3 years old, I was charmed by a snake in the yard. My grandmother came out just in time.

I've really been covered by God, even though I always ran from my anointing. We always had a lot of love in the house. My grandmother would make me these pretty little dresses. She was a seamstress and liked to dress me up. To this day I like pretty clothes because of her.

I didn't know my real dad because of how young my mom was when she had me. All I knew was, he wanted nothing to do with us. He never signed my birth certificate, so my stepfather is the only dad I've ever known. I didn't understand that he wasn't my real father until years later. I never felt like I didn't belong to him, until he started to change towards me.

It started when I was 7 years old. I dreaded the weekends, that's when my stepfather would drink a lot. Even being so young I knew that when Friday came along, it would bring drama in my household. He was abusive to my mom, and I just remember how her screams would make me feel. For a while, my grandmother lived next door when she heard the commotion, she'd charge over. For some reason, my dad would always back down from her.

When she moved across town we had to sneak and call her when the fights would get out of hand. I don't know if it was fear or respect, but my dad never gave my grandmother the energy he gave my mother. Shortly after, my mom got a job where she worked second shifts. My dad would be home in the evenings with us. Around that time, he began touching me.

It started with him taking my hand and putting it on his private parts. I didn't know it was wrong because it made him happy. Usually drinking made him angry, I thought I was just doing something good. As a little girl you just do what you think your father likes. Soon it would turn into touching and fondling me. Never penetrating me but almost.

One night he came into my room. I had siblings that were younger than me, so I always had my own by this time. That night he was on top of me for a little while before I felt warm liquid dripping down my legs. He then got up and told me to wash myself off. Once I started noticing he didn't do it around or with the other children I knew it was wrong. I started to dislike what was going on.

He never took my virginity. I guess rubbing himself on my young body caused him to get aroused enough. My feelings for him changed. I was afraid of him. Not afraid enough to tell, but afraid enough to do what I was told in fear that I'd make him angry enough to go too far. I didn't really know what too far was, but I knew it could be worse than what was already going on. At least that's what I told myself. When he wasn't drinking, he was a great person. He was always a really good cook and he loved to cook the meals we loved to eat. He never treated us badly when he was sober. He was nice to us when he wasn't in his dark place. I think he stopped drinking for a little bit out of guilt for what he was doing to me. It didn't last long.

He would start to take us for rides in the car. It would always be ruined because he would want to teach me how to drive all the time. None of the other children, just me. He would sit me on his lap to teach me. It wouldn't be long before I'd feel his private parts growing and the pumping just enough for the others to overlook what he was doing to me. What would start off as a good day would always end with me feeling confused and disgusted. For a while I assumed my mom knew, and this was just something I was supposed to do. I didn't think telling would change anything. Instead, I started putting on extra layers of clothes at night so he couldn't leave the slimy stuff on my legs when he would rub up against me. I dreaded the weekends.

Every Friday he would come home with his alcohol and let us all lay in the bed with him to watch tv. He would even let us drink a few sips of his beer. When it was time to go to bed, he would make everyone go except me. That's when I really started to know it was wrong, he hid it from everyone.

When I fully realized it was wrong, I was too scared to tell my mom. Not for myself, but for her. I was afraid of what he'd do if she tried to make him stop. He was already beating her. I didn't want him to beat her any more than he already did. I didn't want to be the cause of any fights. I used to lock myself in my closet and cover my ears because things would be so bad.

Looking back, I realize that he was an insecure man. He would accuse her of messing around with people at her job. When she would try to defend herself, he would start beating her. I remember him punching her to the floor while she held my brother in her arms feeding him, all because she didn't make his plate yet.

A couple years later, I finally decided to speak up. I was tired of him doing it, I knew I needed to tell someone. At this time, I was around 10 years old. My brother was the first person I confided in. I made him pinky swear not to tell.

I told him how our dad would do weird things to me. How he'd leave his bodily fluids on me at night. I told him how much I hated it and how disgusted I was by him. My brother kept his promise in not telling. This didn't stop him from advocating for me whenever our dad would try to make everyone else go to bed.

He started speaking up on my behalf, arguing our dad down saying I was just as tired as everyone else. This didn't cause any major changes. He'd walk into my room the second everyone else had fallen asleep.

It's actually what forced me to start layering up. The more clothes I wore, the safer I felt.

My mom did eventually end up finding out about a month after I had told my brother. It was a Saturday; I know that because we cleaned the house on Saturdays. My brother and I were in the room cleaning and my mom were in the kitchen washing the dishes. We started getting into a loud disagreement because he wanted me to make the bed. Since I refused, he resorted to blackmail. I don't think he really planned on telling, he was just doing what siblings do. It was my immediate quietness from shock that caught my mother's attention.

She demanded to know what he was talking about. I instantly started to cry, and, in that moment, my brother told her everything I once told him. She wanted to know why I never told her. I recall the hurt on her face when I had admitted to her that I thought she knew. She was shocked and angry with him.

She grabbed me and told me I didn't do anything wrong. The next thing she did was go into protection mode. All of his things were packed up and put out. She changed the locks so he couldn't get in. It was the day she finally stood up to him. Not for herself, but for her children. That day I realized that my mom would do anything to protect me.

Years later he came back into the home. He never touched me again. A lot of things happened to me because of my childhood trauma. I chose the wrong guys and eventually drug abuse turned me into another person. I'm now clean and married to someone I feel like was sent to me by God. Together we had built a ministry and safe place for people from all walks of life to hear God's word with no judgment.

Trina's story was a massive surprise to me because I didn't know her personally, I just knew of her growing up. I do know that she always stayed to herself. She dressed well and was nice looking but was perceived to be stuck up. She was actually fighting battles alone. This is why this project is so important. You never know what someone else is going through.

The Cost Of Being An "It Girl"

Trina

My name is Trina Gale. My story almost reads like Tyler Perry's "The Haves and Have Nots." I grew up in two households at different times in my life. My parents were young when I was born. My mom being 16 and my father 19. They were both exploring and trying to figure out life. I was the only child on both sides for about 7 years.

My mother raised me up until the age of ten. We lived on the south side of town in the Southbridge projects. My mother ruled with a heavy voice, and a heavier hand. You did what she said, nothing else. I was in an alcoholic environment with her. She struggled with it until the last year of her life.

She was broken to which I didn't understand until later on in my own life. Going through my own hard struggles, and internal work.

My father was always in my life since day one. He's kind and soft spoken. He's the kind of guy that everyone likes. He grew up surrounded by his family. When I was with my dad, I was daddy's girl and wherever he went I went. So, I was always around family. My parents partied, and with partying came alcohol. Whenever I reminisce with my father about the good ole days, he always reminds me that I was a beer baby. I was drinking beer in the womb, and I would drink beer before I would drink milk. My father stopped drinking and has been sober for years now. At the tender age of around 10 years old until I was 19 years old, I lived with my father and now stepmother. To whom I affectionally refer to as my parents. I now lived in a house, my own room, my own telephone line, and 2 working parents. That new plush life meant I had to share my dad to which I wasn't accustomed to. Raising me wasn't for the faint at heart because I intentionally gave them a tough time. Going from daddy's girl to daddy's brat in an instant. Today with that same intention I make sure to thank them and most importantly thank the woman who chose to raise someone else's problemed child. Today sharing comes easily, I have siblings on both sides of my blended family 2 brothers and 2 sisters. As a child and into my adult years, I struggled with acceptance issues, so I was reserved. People often saw that as indication that I thought I was all that but quite the contrary I thought nothing of myself. Before the age of 13 I was exposed to nudity I would find nude magazines or flash cards at family member's house. Unbeknownst to them I would steal away every chance I got to see these items because now my young mind was curious about the bodies that I see on those cards or magazines as I held them with gazing eyes. I hoped that one day the same changes would happen to my undeveloped body. As time went on, I elevated my curiosity and began watching porn. When I watched porn, I now had a feeling. My body was feeling things in areas I wasn't sure of and not ready for. From that point on I was interested in sex but not active at that time. As I began to make friends and began to stay over family members' homes something different started happening. The males started to take notice in me, and the private groping sessions started. Even my childhood girlfriend started to take notice in me, but I kept quiet like a good girl should, or so I thought. As I grappled with this in my adult years, I often wondered did I exhibit some sort of behavior to make any of them think this was ok. I never enjoyed the groping but had become accustomed to being used in that way. I used to cringe whenever the adults would leave because I knew the window of opportunity was wide open, and it was time for me to be used. I would stand there staring off into space until it was over. These instances occurred for a few years but finally stopped. I still cringe when I'm touched, I must process the thought of being touched. I blamed myself for years for being "fast" as the old folks called it. I became promiscuous and as an adult I feel those encounters have altered my idea of intimacy. For years I wore that note from my childhood. It was pinned to my chest by everyone person who used me asking, "Who wants to use me next?" Now I'm in a new intimidating life, a new intimidating neighborhood, with new intimidating people. I stayed around the house in the beginning and my father would encourage me to go out and make some friends so that I did. I began to come out my shell, I was with the "it" girls so that had to make me an "it" girl, right? I finally felt accepted, approved, and validated. With those credentials I started to get attention from the boys. Only the "it" girls can garner the attention I was starting to receive.

In my father's house I couldn't date until I was 16. That was his only rule. A whole lot of sneaking around took place. Throughout the years of friendship, laughter, and running the streets the bomb eventually dropped. The "it" girls were never my friends. My need for total acceptance made me an easy target, I was put on the block.

My friend had influence so what she said was concrete. If she said I was bad news then trust, I was bad news without the benefit of the doubt. All connections I thought I developed through this friendship were a lie. Boys were encouraged to go after me. Again, I was experiencing and allowing the routine of being used to continue. The rumors been to roll of the press. Some rumors were true to the period on a sentence but in some of those rumors were a complete set of lies. I'm forever grateful to the two young ladies who seen me and went against the words that were being said about me. They pulled me to the side and told me exactly what my friend was saying, and my narrow mind began to see things differently.

The friendships dissolved and I found myself alone. I'd be the first to admit I didn't know the first thing about being a friend, but I never went against the grain of that friendship. I began wandering about making friends here and there. I tried friendships with the squares, the cliques, the educated, the uneducated.

 Still never finding that place of security in a friendship. I had begun to expect things to fall apart from the beginning and started to self-sabotage. I was to needy and yet not willing to give. I believed that in the back of people's mind, they didn't forget what they assumed they knew. I convinced myself that people didn't want to be associated with someone labeled like me. It was too much to risk and I wasn't worth the risk for with every new friendship came judgement. It was always about the man.

I secluded myself emotionally which brought about a loneliness that I couldn't shake and an insecurity I couldn't face. Now where in the 1990's and the scene is starting to change. The hustlers and drug dealers of my time are on the set. I seen lifestyles changed by this. I wanted a part of it. I know the familiar part," being used "I did that while staring into space I know I could do it for a lifestyle change. I was too busy having fun as a teenager, I didn't have a plan, idea or thought other than that. I couldn't hold a halfway intelligent conversation and didn't have a clue about a relationship. The issue was that the big-time dealers had main chicks so I would be the side chick with no benefits. I began to think my pipe dream would never happen. Until that one day a young handsome fellow approached me. I had just gotten my own project housing in the Eastlake extension, and I had never seen him around that way before. In my mind it was all good because he doesn't know about me yet so let me act fast. In a matter of time, it became obvious to me that this young man was starting to make a name in the streets, and he liked me. We began to form a relationship of some sorts, me not knowing how to be in a relationship and him not being in many relationships at the time in his life but we managed. Shortly thereafter the lifestyle I dreamed of started to happen before my eyes. You couldn't have told me I wasn't in the best time and place in my life. His name got bigger, his pockets got fatter, and the dynamics changed. Just like myself there where 5 women on every corner that desired that same lifestyle. Envy quickly came into play. I was hated in a neighborhood where mostly everyone was born and raised so they had earned their stripes. I'm an outsider by all standards and code. How dare an outsider to date one of the biggest names in the game.

Not long into the relationship I felt I wasn't getting the glory and bells a drug dealers girl deserves. I stole a package and hid it and that was the day I'll never forget and the day the abuse started, and I thought would never end. How could I be so greed stricken, how could someone who never got anything think she deserved more.

The drug dealing illusion had me caught up, bound, and now getting abused. If I was big enough to steal, then I must have brought this on myself and deserved every bit of it. The abuse escalated; I had a three-way system going on constantly! Physical, mental, and emotional all upside my head at any given moment. I totally lost myself and forgot who I was. The person I loved was also the person I feared. Fear is an understatement he was the person I was terrified of. I was called a female dog as my first name, and I would never be let to live down the fact that I was a whore. At this point it was easy for me to assume all my years where at my doorstep. He now knows me. I believe he hated that, and he was well known and respected to be with someone like me.

The abuse started to show itself in front of outsiders and I finally had enough and began fighting back. I had already been beaten, spit on, and lied to so I made an escape plan. I began to steal again slowly this time; I wouldn't be that fool to steal big twice. Thinking I would have a nest for when he was gone but he had the loyalty of many, and that plan was derailed in the early stages. The only thing I had left was to knuckle up every time he did. I was broken so what was one more black eye, or busted lip? What was one more time waking up on the floor unaware you were even hit? It was nothing! But I was exhausted, so I had to go to plan B through Z. It was my last hope before that one hit killed me. I went to the housing authority and make an appealing plea.

I don't recall what story line I used but I know it worked. It had to be God. I asked the housing manager to board the house but leave the backdoor clear. I must have said I needed to get something out of the house for that to have happened. But I stayed in the house while it was boarded. The rumors starting swirling in the projects. Some thought I was under police protection, so thought I was evicted. The only though that mattered to me was the abuser thought. He also felt it was something to do with the police. From that day he never wanted to step foot in that house for the simple fact that the police would be watching him. By God's grace and mercy, I was set free. There were a few small hiccups here and there and he wanted to use that same hand but at that point that hand had no control over me.

Thankfully since that season in my life I was blessed with a chance of true love. Someone who heard it all and still chose me. I didn't quite understand what was being offered and didn't know how to give it back. But I'll never forget that feeling and the look of love in somebody's eyes.

I hold that person dear in my heart until the end. I now am in a wonderful place in my life. I was able to pick up the pieces of me, heal the little girl inside, and move on. I began by forgiving myself and asking others to forgive me. I started soul searching because I was tired of carrying the heavy load of my past. My shadow was large and overwhelming, and I couldn't outrun it with my best sneakers on. I tried leaving the state I was born and raised in but came to find out I took me wherever I went. I had the proclivities to meet people even when I wasn't available but my low self-esteem, and broken spirit would run them off as well. I knew I had to heal the seat of my soul I started with positive affirmations. Which was hard for me because I never heard a positive thing about me. I had the hardest time hearing myself say these positive, uplifting, encouraging words. My stomach would turn every time I attempted to say these things to myself. But I said to myself, "self" no more of this. I told my sub conscious to get in order you work for me. I then began to agree with myself that I AM whatever I choose to be. And I choose to be my most authentic self, to exercise kindness, and to believe in me and show up for me.

That I AM enough for the world and if the world doesn't agree then that's the worlds problem. I continually work on my shadow, and it has receded some. My big toe is out and that's a start. To that I can smile and hold my head high. The rest is history! I encourage anyone dealing with abuse, insecurities, low self-esteem find the courage in you and make that first step. Seek therapy and plan your escape route. I might not happen the first time but be not dismayed. Keep pushing and you will break through. Know that you are worth it, that you deserve it, and you are loved.

Peace and Blessings

Ciara

As a kid I always knew I was creative, but I didn't know the level of my creativeness. My father made me want to possibly become a writer of some sort but since I wasn't sure I just decided to try a few other things first. I would say watching my dad inspired me to tap into the creative side with writing. My mother is an expert cosmetologist, so I'm surrounded by creativity.

I had a great childhood, but it wasn't always perfect. I experienced things like my parents divorcing etc. Not knowing all of this was molding me into who I am today. Soon after my parents' divorce, I started focusing on writing short pieces and other things. No, I wasn't the best, but I was able to get things together on paper. By the time I graduated, I had written a children's book that I never published. Now that my kids are older, I may revise it and publish it for them. Regardless, again I've always been into writing but sometimes life throws us curve balls and we go astray.

Moving on, I graduated and went to work. I decided to date my husband and those dreams and ambitions sort of dwindled. It's a battle when you're just trying to survive so I didn't focus on anything creative. Unfortunately, this made life harder for me because I always needed to write something. Life happened and I lost myself trying to make everyone happy. Definitely a dark moment because I didn't realize how important I was and still am. Not to be arrogant by far but I'm glad I snapped out of it because I've been able to hear wonderful things and become a part of even greater projects. One day, I had an open vision about my magazine. Not sure of where to even start, I begin to do research because I'm a person that needs to see numbers. I can hear you all day long but if I'm not seeing the numbers it won't matter about what you're telling me. I guess in a way, I've had trust issues. Lol I think we all have those type of problems where it was simply hard to trust people.

Either way, over the years it's developed who I am. I went from seeing myself as not super strong to be extraordinarily strong because I got over those trust issues and really took God at His word concerning my life. Something happens when you decide to trust God. He developed me and is still doing that. I'm very human. I love seeing other people succeed and I love to help them get there. Sometimes, I may help too much but it's ok right?

Either way fast forwarding to today, I'm not only creating magazines, but I'm also coaching, writing more, and creating more. I've accepted the word creative over my life. There's no more struggle with trying to figure out if I'm creative or not. I know that for sure. I'm grounded in knowing that finally. It to say that I don't struggle with that but sometimes even that title can be draining. The older I get, the more familiar I'm becoming with the word NO. It took some time to get there because one of my flaws is that I care lol. In all seriousness, I'm grateful to go through the things that I have. It's become a part of my evolution.

As a woman I aspire to be able to touch others and become a role model. I never thought I would say that, but I've been able to learn a few gems and try my best to live as being that good person. Something that I learned from all of this is that you should never try to be anyone but yourself and learn to be gentle with your evolution of self. If you know you're supposed to be doing something else, don't push it off. Make it happen. Sacrifices will pay off. That's just how life falls. Another lesson I learned is that you can't be everything to everyone. Learn to say no and be ok with your decision but also, I've learned to never let opportunities pass you by. In chasing the journey of real success, chase God before anything. That's the first lesson I learned. God first and other things will follow. The people will follow. Do God first. You'll be fine and you will win. I live by this!

This young lady has a story that we all can relate to. Everyone has felt alone some time in their life.

Isolated

Raevyn Sarai

We all get anxious sometimes. We all get the overwhelming feeling of stress and endless worrying. We don't share it with others, we keep it within. We don't always realize how bad it can be for us or how bad it may be for others. We may not even realize how much it changes you. Personally, I suffered from social anxiety.

There was a time where I actually enjoyed being around kids my age.

When I was eight, I used to like being outside, I went to the park, I went places with people, and I walked into stores with no problem. I've never been

the most talkative person, but I was willing to try.
I've always had regular anxiety. I'm usually anxious
when it comes to adults. I have an overwhelming
fear of coming off as disrespectful towards any of
my elders. I've always broken down into tears
whenever any adult who wasn't my mother raised
their voice at me.

My social anxiety came around the ages of 10-11. It
was the rudeness of kids that started everything for
me. In fifth grade I went to an all-African American
school, I'm on the darker side. I don't think I've
ever had a problem with my skin before then. My 8-
year-old friends and I never made colored jokes
about each other, so when it started happening in a
school filled with people who looked just like me, I
didn't really know how to manage it.

Kids who were supposed to be my friends would
often throw in a disrespectful comment about how
dark I was. I even had a "friend" who'd call me

"Gorilla" and said it was a nickname she was going to call me. I knew the difference between friend insults and full-on disrespect, so it was things like that which gave me reasons to not want to open up or be around anyone my age. That caused me to become anxious about going to school. I loved doing schoolwork and learning about new things, I just no longer enjoyed the fact that I had to be in a classroom full of kids in order to do it.

I got so psyched out about having to deal with people that I went to the nurse and said something that I'm not even sure I meant. I told my school nurse I wanted to take scissors and cut my throat open. Now that I'm older, I honestly don't think I necessarily wanted to kill myself. I was never the type to spend days or even hours thinking about how I didn't want to be on earth. In fact, life always seemed good until it was time for me to go to school. I feel like I was so upset with being in a classroom full of people that in the heat of the moment it was the only thing I could think about. I was forced to spend time in a treatment program, when I completed it, they placed me on homebound for the rest of the school year. It honestly helped me. I was inpatient for only 7 days; I attended their outpatient program for around 3 months. I spent the rest of my middle/high school years going in between treatment programs and homeschooling. This program actually saved me, I was in an environment with a certain amount of people, I could still get my schoolwork done, and I was also working on my mental state in the process. The problem is, I started getting comfortable with running to them whenever I wasn't ready to deal with school. It became unhealthy. I was no longer going outside to try and make friends. I was no longer doing simple things like walking into stores by myself. I was no longer comfortable having conversations with people. I realized I would never be able to force myself to step out of my comfort zone if I were constantly going to this treatment center to shield me. I decided to talk to my mom about going to one-on-one therapy sessions. All my mom wanted was for me to live my childhood. She loved that I stayed out of the streets, but she hated that I was wasting my time. The new therapist we got wanted to work on forcing me to be uncomfortable. She'd make me have sessions in public places. She'd have me do something I wouldn't normally be comfortable with. We had goals that she wanted me to achieve.

This therapist helped me get through a lot. She's a big part of how I made it to college in the first place. I've worked on overcoming a lot since 5th grade. I'm a first-year student in college now. I'm not the best at carrying conversations and I still struggle to make friends. However, I'm not the same person I was 2 years ago. I wasn't sure if I'd even make it to college because of how hard it was to stay committed to public school throughout the years. I proved myself and my anxiety wrong. I will always be proud of that, and I will continue to manage it better. I no longer want to hold myself back, nor do I want to miss out on anything else and I don't plan to.

When I was 13 years old my mother, who is a published author, you may have heard of her…K.D. Harris, she encouraged me to turn my journal into a book. I released, *Exceptionally Weird: Embrace your Uniqueness* and it became an Amazon's best seller in two days. My goal was to encourage other young people who may have Anxiety.

This next author isn't new to the book world at all. In fact, her name might ring bells. You may have read one of her many novels, if not you may have heard of them. She's the writer of Poison, the Bliss series, Beautiful Demise, and an entire catalog of novels. She was blessed with awards for the Best-Selling Author and has even ghost written for some of your favorite reality tv stars. The story she decided to share was one she tried to shy away from. If it weren't for her overcoming her pride, I don't think she would've gotten the courage to share with us the truth behind the scenes. But she did, and maybe it'll reach the right people.

Pride was my downfall

K.D. Harris

When this anthology was presented to me, I thought it was an impressive idea; women from all diverse levels of society coming together to share a snippet of their own personal accounts of healing and discovery of oneself.

I was raised in the Christian belief, and it was always said that we suffer so that our testimony could help someone else. I embraced that. So, when trials and tribulations would come my way, I would remember that this will not last, and this is not for me, it's for someone else. My job was to encourage others and tell them how I made it through. However, I did no such thing.

I was raised by my paternal great-grandmother until the age of three. She became ill and could no longer take care of me nor her home which was conjoined with the infamous corner store, "Cliff's" on eighth street over on the east side of Wilmington. She moved into a high-rise called the *Windsor*. An "old folks" home, at least that's what my friends and I called it. I was then sent to live with her daughter and stayed in her home until I was eighteen.

My great-grandmother made sure that I had the top of the line when it came to materials. The grandmother whom I lived with did the bare minimum. I learned early to rely on myself and become self-sufficient. They were both entrepreneurs. They owned restaurants, daycare centers and dabbled in a little bit of everything.

My grandmother was one of the very few black people in Brookmont Farms who owned their home. I had no idea what section 8 was. The only thing I was familiar with was Food Stamps. We received them because she was taking care of my two cousins and me. That was the only proof of poverty that I was aware of. I did not meet my birth mother until I was seventeen years old. I knew nothing of her or her family because she was forbidden. Years later I would find out that my great-grandmother stole me from her when I was eight months old. She did not fit in their mold. She was given an ultimatum and was forced from my life. She was only sixteen years old.

As you can see my family was something else. A high yellow clan of women who looked down on others who were not on their level. So, it was inevitable that my chunky chocolate skin self would have all types of inner insecurities. The thing is I would never show it. Weakness was not allowed. I had to be strong. Successful and failure was not an option. For the most part I was just that. There were a few bumps along the way, but it didn't matter because there were six figures in my bank account.

In 2007, my great-grandmother passed away. Due to false truths, I found out concerning my birth mother, I was not on the best terms with her. However, she was still my rock, and I did not understand life without her. A few months after her death I met a guy. He was decent. He had money, he was business minded like me and he was gorgeous. I had just signed my first major publishing deal for my book *Poison*. This guy was in the entertainment industry. He was a rapper, so he knew all about marketing and getting noticed.

I collaborated with him for a while, and we helped each other grow in our businesses. He understood the marketing and I knew the business side. I was an owner of a childcare center, and I was bringing in well over ten thousand dollars a month. For me to be a single parent and homeowner I was doing great for myself.

Our relationship flourished. I did something I vowed to never do and that was bring him around my children. I was very overprotective with my children because I was told that I would never birth a child. I was blessed with two, so they meant everything to me. A year later my uncle contested my great-grandmother's will. She was listed as the owner of my home, so I had to sell it. I was so upset because I turned my garage into my center. I was losing my business. Instead of fighting, I walked away from everything and focused on my writing career.

My friend was by my side the entire time. He helped me find an apartment for all of us in Newark. I ended up going to work at Comcast which was the first job I had since I was twenty-two. I was thirty-three years old at that time. It was a huge change for me. I went from six figures a year to making twenty-six thousand. I was ok because I had plenty of money in the bank. My goal was to eventually buy a building and open a center. That took a back seat because I was flourishing in the book game.

His mother ended up being my children's babysitter. This is when things hit the fan. One day I was over at her house finishing up the sequel to Poison. A dark-skinned woman with glasses walked in carrying a baby seat. All eyes were on me. She stared at me like she wanted to kill me. She introduced herself as my friend's wife. The six-month-old baby in the carriage was their son. I had to play it cool because there was no way that I was going to allow her to get under my skin. I smiled and said hi. I turned back to my book as if she were not there. Not paying her dust. I looked at that as strength. I would never allow anyone to knock me off of my block.

That evening when he came home to our house, I confronted him. He had an amazing story saying that he only married her so she could get a green card. His mother co-signed the story and I believed it. Months went on and we were closer than ever. His guard dropped and I found out something about him that I never knew. He was a gambler. I mean super addicted to gambling. At this point in the relationship, we were sharing money. I didn't think anything of it because he made sure I was driving nice vehicles. We went out on dates; he was spoiling me with jewelry. I was used to doing things for myself. I always had wonderful things. I was not hung up on the material gifts, it was the fact that he was doing this for me.

I was always on the heavier side. During this time, I was at my highest weight. I was wearing a size twenty-six. He never made me feel bad about my size nor did he try to make me change. He loved me for me. My kids loved him. It had gotten to the point that I allowed him to manage all of the bills and money since he was "the man" and it was his job to take care of us.

One night I was working late at my job. Security came to my cubicle and said I needed to come out front with them. I did not know what was going on. When we got outside my vehicle was sitting on a tow truck. It was being repossessed because I was four months behind. I was beyond confused. I called him immediately and there was no answer. I had a breakdown because for once in my life I did not know how to fix it. I was embarrassed. Everyone was watching my car being taken out of the window. I refused to go back upstairs. I had them bring me my stuff. My supervisor took me home and the next day I took a leave of absence for six months.

When he arrived home three days later, he looked like death. His eyes were bloodshot red. His locks were wild. He had the same clothes on from the last time I saw him. I wanted to go in on him, but I could not. He looked defeated. He sat on the side of the bed and tears fell. I rushed to his side asking what was wrong. He kept saying he had a problem and he needed help. I automatically thought he had a drug issue. I asked him what he was on, I told him I would help him through it. He looked up to me and said, "I have a gambling problem."

I wanted to slap the hell out of him. Gambling. I thought he was joking. I started yelling and cursing him out. I wanted him to leave. Eventually he did. For two weeks straight I laid in my bed sick. I could not sleep. I did not want to do anything. I didn't even want to pray. I felt as if God had forsaken me. I was so caught up in my new life that God had taken a back seat. I still went to church, but I felt stupid because I let my guard down and allowed a man to bring me down. I ended up taking Ambien, a sleep drug because I did not want to be awake. He ended up coming back. He had won over fifty thousand dollars and purchased me a car. I was still not going to work. I was too embarrassed. My bills were behind because my money was low. I had a little over fifteen thousand dollars to my name.

One night we were in bed, and I was awakened by high beamed lights shining through my window. I woke him up and he jumped up immediately. He ran to our closet and retrieved a gun. I had no idea that he had weapons in the house with my kids. I jumped up and went to my kids room. I opened the door and there were five red beams reflecting on their covers. My life felt like it was going to end. There were men at my patio door with guns and at the front door. We were surrounded. I answered the door and begged them not to do anything to my children. The men were Jamaican, and I was always told they did not play. They saw that I had nothing to do with it, but they wanted their money. He owed them sixty thousand dollars. They took what he had. I promised them that I would empty out my account that next morning if they would let my kids live. They stayed in front of my house all night. That next morning. I removed all of my money and gave them a cashier's check. I lost it all.

I did not tell anyone what happened because of my pride, and I had to stay strong. I ended up staying in my house with no electricity. No hot water, but I refused to ask for help. My eight-year-old daughter was going to the deli to charge my phone. My children stuck by my side. They did not mind eating sandwiches and chips every night for dinner. They got used to the cold water and candles for warmth and light. After two weeks I made the ultimate sacrifice. I called my aunt in North Carolina and asked if she could take my children for a while. She took them with no questions asked.

I wanted to die. He stayed with me for a while longer until the pills took over me. I was hoping that God would just take me in my sleep. He eventually went back to his wife because I became dependent on the sleeping pills and Xanax. Two months into my depression, a friend from my church got tired of me ignoring her. She pulled up and checked in on me. When she saw the condition, I was in she forced me to leave. I left everything behind.

I got my kids back a month later and went back to work. I started to write again. It took several years for me to get back on my feet. I had to learn that I had to trust God. No man or amount of money could give me what I needed. I have not reached the financial level that I was at before however I know that in God's time I will rise again.

It's okay to be strong but do not allow pride to get in the way. I believe this was the start to my humbling season. I was prideful. It was instilled in me that I didn't need anyone, and I had to face things on my own. I thought I suffered alone. The truth is, I was never alone. God was with me the entire time. That's why I'm here today. I can say that I have changed, however God is still working with me. I learned that we can still be strong and accept help. When we are prideful is when we are actually weak.

When I first spoke to Aisha, I could feel her positive energy through the phone. Once I interviewed her and learned more about her story, I knew it was a subject that needed to be a part of this book. It may be one of the most important and common issues women of color deal with…COLORISM

Pretty, For A Dark-Skinned Girl

Aisha

56 Batista Street was a busy household. It stood the third of many single-family houses on a small residential street. It was just off a main road filled with bodegas, liquor stores, Chinese shops, all types of people, and crime. Inside, my family consisted of two very loving and overly supportive black parents. My mother, the youngest of eight, and her family had migrated from Georgia in the 70's. Meanwhile my father, the youngest of five, and his family came from Alabama.

Both of my parents had children in their teenage years before they met each other. My father entered their relationship with four children, 3 of whom had different mothers. While my mother entered with two children by 2 different men. Similarly, to their family dynamics, I was born into a blended family of six children. My dad's two oldest were boys, they didn't come around much. His daughters, on the other hand, were there almost every weekend and summer.

They lived on the other side of town with their grandmother and their siblings. As I was the only child my parents shared, it made me the most fortunate amongst us all. It also made me the black sheep. I had a different relationship with each sibling, although I wouldn't say one was better than the other. All strained in their own way due to circumstances that occurred way before I was even born.

Maybe I could have accepted the nickname, "The Black Sheep,'" but those were not the chosen names of endearment that they'd use to refer to me. Instead, I was the fat, the black, or the ugly one on some days, Bertha Butt on others. When they were being silly, or entertaining their friends and neighborhood kids, my siblings would join in on the jokes about my "Bertha Butt." They would sometimes change it up and refer to me as "Bertha Butt Boogie," named after my mother's close girlfriend Bertha. Big Bertha as they'd call her. It wasn't long before their friends were comfortable joining in on the jokes to alter my name.

All three of my sisters could've passed for my mother's daughters. While they were varying shades of yellow, their French vanilla complexions and long black hair was no comparison to my rich brown skin and ashy brown kinks that couldn't skip the iconic hot comb treatment on the mornings of Easter Sundays.

My oldest sister, the artist, was the identical twin of my mother. Although she was five feet 7 inches tall, her long legs and slim frame made her appear much taller. Her naturally curly hair fell all the way down her back, but it was her almond shaped eyes and long eyelashes that stood out to the crowd. A natural beauty, she instantly became the fantasy in the dreams of all the teenage boys in the city.

Sister number 2, the oldest of my dad's girls and his first true love, was only about five feet tall but her boldly shaped body was described by many as an eight-ball figure. Often mistaken for someone of the Latina descent, many studied her features in search of her true nationality. Her complexion, the fairest skinned tone of all the girls, symbolized to most outside observers that she could not be a black girl. I felt a rare connection with sister number 3, at times close but at other times distant enough to be a stranger. She was the sister who was closer to my age, and something about her features were different from the other two. While she was more of an olive skin tone, she was never mistakenly called brown or any tone that would insinuate that she could be darker than the others.

There was one boy out of us 5, the golden child. A multi-faced athlete who was just as talented in football, as he was in baseball. He was tall and slim, his skin a russet, reddish brown. His eyes, a bold green that would change to hazel at the drop of a dime.

When people saw me with my siblings, it would be as if they'd seen a ghost. "That's your sister too?" or "The black one is your sister?" are just some of the statements of shock that their friends would throw out every time I showed up.

Few dark-skinned black women visited 56 Batista Street. Not many dark-skinned people in general. Except for Abigail Dolly, my cabbage patch baby, that I would bring with me everywhere. Abigail's complexion wasn't dark either, actually she was a white cabbage patch doll, but in my play world, she was my daughter, and her father was of Hispanic descent. I can remember tying t-shirts around my head and pretending that I had long blonde hair like Abigail, as we enjoyed our daily routine of imaginary play.

I guess I never really did notice that I had blossomed from fat, black, and ugly to "pretty for a dark-skinned girl." Maybe it was because the compliment did not fill the hole in my soul. It was something about those words that would echo through my mind, just like when they'd call me all those other not so friendly names. No matter how it was phrased, it felt as if the compliment was taken away just as quickly as it was given. I can still see my mother's friends, as they rubbed the side of my round cheeks with the palm of their hand, proudly telling me how pretty I was to be so dark. Other times, I wasn't quite pretty, sometimes just cute, but even still that couldn't be a compliment in itself either. "For a dark-skinned girl" always followed behind what would've been a compliment.

I still remember the day that someone saw me beyond my skin complexion, as if it were yesterday. It was the summer right before my 14th birthday. Standing five feet 4 inches tall, my now permed hair hung down the middle of my back. I wore it out in a hairstyle that we'd refer to as a Doobie, a title given to the hair style by the Dominican women who moved from New York City to set up salons in Connecticut.

"Oh wait, I didn't even introduce myself to you! Is this session only 1 hour? I guess you want to know who I am and why I'm here for therapy? My name is Aisha, and although I'm inclined to tell you that my name is Aisha Lawrence and I have a master's in management and organizational leadership, so that you don't judge me as an undereducated dark skin black girl, I should at least tell you my first name!"

"Hi, Aisha. It's nice to meet you, my name is Jane. Yes, your session is only for an hour, but we can meet more often if you need to. You can continue with where you left off."

"Where was I? Oh yes, I was telling you about Shawn." Shawn was the first person to make me feel pretty. All the girls in the city wanted Shawn. Shawn and his older brother moved to Connecticut from New York City to live with their aunt when their parents were sent to prison for

Cocaine Distribution. While their father had twenty-two kids, Shawn and Dave were their mother's only 2 children who were now her sister, Susie's responsibility. Shawn and Dave were selling drugs for their parents since they were nine. Although only an hour away from New York City, Connecticut was easy money to them because the demand was high and the supply low. With their New York connections still intact, they were able to triple their profits in the cities in Connecticut.

I remember the first day I met Shawn like it was yesterday. He was driving a white BMW 745. My oldest sister would always say, "there goes the boy with the quarter to 8", but I didn't really understand what that meant.

My sisters and I were walking to the corner store, when he drove past us and then stopped and put his car in reverse.

"Excuse me, beautiful, what's your name?" Shawn asked. Unlike them, I kept walking, because I didn't have time for boys. But as I kept walking, he put his car in park and got out to catch up with me. "Excuse me, beautiful, what's your name?" Shawn asked again. "Are you talking to me?" I responded. "I'm nowhere near as beautiful as you are, so I can't be talking to myself. What's your name, can I take you out to eat?" Shawn asked.

Knowing that my parents would never let me go out on a date with a boy who drove a car more expensive than their house, and because my sisters were acting as if Shawn had committed a major crime by stopping to talk to me, I kept walking and went into the store to get my quarter water and sour powers, but what I felt inside I could not explain.

Over the next year, Shawn and his crew had made a reputation for themselves. By this time, he had 3 or

4 different cars, but I quickly learned every detail of every car he owned, although I still hadn't said many words to Shawn. Even though it seems that everywhere I went, Shawn would mysteriously show up, I didn't think that he would really choose me over all the prettier girls in our city.

The summer of my 10th grade in school, I had enrolled at a summer program to earn college credits and was waiting to catch the bus to the mall to go shopping for my stay. As I waited for the bus, a Lexus ES 300 pulled up to the bus stop. When the window rolled down, it was Shawn, and he said to me, "Get In!" That was the Beginning to No End!

The next two years we spent almost every minute we could together. Shawn would spoil me with lavish gifts. Gucci, Fendi, Louis Vuitton, you name it he bought it. But the Jeep Grand Cherokee LTD that he purchased for me for my high school graduation was by far the most beautiful gift he could have gotten me. Graduating number 16 in a class of 286 students, I got accepted into Florida A&M, Spellman University, and even Howard University, but somehow, I was able to convince my parents into letting me stay home and attend our local State College. There was no way I was going to leave Shawn and move South. Although we had some issues with infidelity, and he even had a baby during our relationship, I knew that I was lucky to have Shawn. It's not like I could find someone better, Shawn saw me like no one else did!

I enrolled at one of our 4 State colleges, majoring in Business. Although I went to school in Connecticut, as the only one of my mother's children to attend college, college was important to my mom, so I lived on campus. College was a defining moment in my life, because it was in college that I met some of my closest friends, and even some nice guys. However, the nice guy couldn't compete with the lifestyle I was used to having after dating Shawn for the past 2 years.

While on Christmas break from school, I had come down with the flu. Shawn was missing in action, during his frequent periods of infidelity, and I was staying with my parents during the school break. After 2 weeks of being sick, my mother made me go to the doctor, and I found out that I was pregnant, 8 weeks to be exact. Afraid, nervous, and in shock, were just a few of the many emotions going through my brain. Although the next 7 months were challenging, I finished my sophomore year of college, right before my baby boy, SJ, was born.

SJ and Shawn were inseparable from the beginning. Like my first encounter with Shawn, SJ loved him at first sight. Shawn's help with SJ made it easy for me to go back to school. While SJ and Shawn grew closer together, Shawn and I were growing further apart. I'm not sure if James had anything to do with the distance growing between Shawn and I, but I'm sure that meeting James during my last year of college didn't help.

James was the opposite of Shawn, a silly and innocent basketball player and Engineer major from Baltimore, Maryland, his southern drawl instantly stood out. Although he was an Engineer major, James seemed to be in all my classes or anywhere I was at, to say the least. James did not own a car and was not able to take me on trips, out to dinner, or on lavish vacations, but it was as if he saw me for me. James couldn't understand what I saw in Shawn. He was always pressing me about the dangers of Shawn's fast lifestyle and couldn't understand why I didn't see that I deserved so much more. But I didn't have it in me to tell him that I always felt that Shawn deserved more than what I could give him.

The night before graduation, my friends and I were going out to celebrate! Shawn and I had gotten into an argument because he didn't understand why James was going out with the girls, but it was Shawn who always seemed to have issues with cheating, not I, so I ignored his rants and kept on getting dressed. My Dad had picked SJ up that morning, and I was not about to let Shawn ruin my night of celebrating my accomplishments.

We went to three clubs that night, and although my feet were sore, I refused to take off my Louboutin heels. I got home a little after 4:00am., and Shawn was not home. While strange, it wasn't unusual because we had an argument before I had left. Knowing Shawn, he was using this argument to spend some time with his side girl, April or whatever her name was. I was asleep for what felt like 5 minutes, when I was awakened by my phone.

Checking to see if it was Shawn, when I saw my sister's number, I let it go to voicemail. But she instantly called back, and I thought about SJ, and picked up. When I answered, all I could hear was her screams, and I knew what was coming next was not good news. Still, that could not prepare me for what she said.

"They killed him, Aisha, Shawn's Dead," is all I could remember.
Riiiinnnnnnggg!!! The alarm went off. "That's the end of our session today," said Jane.
~Aisha D. Lawrence, MS, MOL

Colorism, the silent soul killer. The blight of Colorism in the African American communities was for many years an untold story. While many watched slave movies, Roots to be exact, documenting the differing experiences of the slave that worked in the house versus outside in the field, for most the unceasing significance of associating lighter skin with being better mirrors the same undertone as racism. It is my hope that through my words, I will not only touch the souls of those beautiful women and girls who are not able to see their beauty beyond the undertone of "for dark skin," just as much as I touch those who cannot identify with the feeling. Because it is through the act of coming together as one that we begin to change the narrative for all

Stephanie's story is a story of survival.

House of Chaos

Stephanie

My name is Stephanie Reeves. I was born and raised in Wilmington Delaware. I'm the mother of six beautiful children and 9 grandchildren. I want to give you all a glimpse into my life. I'm hoping that someone somewhere can relate to my story and look forward to my book of short stories coming the first of the year.

I represent the girl who's been through a lot of pain. For years I never knew what being in a peaceful environment for an extended period of time even felt like. I've had moments of peace but as quickly as the moment came it left. I grew up amongst Chaos. Drugs, Domestic Violence, and death has become something I got use to growing up. Because of that prayer had been something I learned to live by.

I was raised on the eastside of Wilmington. My dad side of the family lived on 11th street where I spent most of my time. My mom had four kids. Me and my youngest brother have the same dad and my oldest sister and brother have the same dad. My mom and dad had this weird toxic relationship. My dad had other children but for a while I only really knew my sister. Although we were really close growing up our mothers were not. For years they fought and argued over my dad. I don't think it ever interfered in our relationship. I just remembered feeling said when they would go at it because I knew my sister wouldn't be able to come over. We were told to stay out of grown folk business, so we never asked questions, but I always wondered why they were so mad at each other and not my dad. My siblings and I are around the same age, so I guess my dad messed around with some of these women at the same time. I think he went back and forth with my sister and my mom.

I remembered spending a lot of time at my dad's mom's house growing up. All my cousins, uncles, and aunts would be there. Back then it was about family. Although my dad dealt with other women you could tell that my mom was considered to be a part of the family and he and my mom had a more committed relationship than he had with my other siblings' mothers or the other women he dealt with at least at that time. To his family Rosey and Cliff were one and my mom was like another one of my grandparents' children. She was family.

My grandfather had a story on the corner of 11th and Kirkwood and my grandmother's house sat on the very next corner on 11th and Spruce. My grandparents were from the south, so they had a different type of hospitality. My grandmother Annie Ruth was always cooking or baking a cake. The house always smelled of a home cooked meal. Because the family was so big, she would always cook a lot of food. She was the type that showed her love through acts of service, so she always wanted us to enjoy a home cooked meal or a baked good. Sweet potato pies, homemade pound cake, banana pudding. Chick, fish, ham hocks and beans. The real definition of soul food. Only thing I hated was that she would make us eat vegetables. Fresh vegetables or not, I didn't want to eat vegetables back then. I can still hear her voice like it was yesterday. 'Gal come in here to get you get yourself something to eat. You hungry ain't cha" She was the rock in the family she kept my dad and his siblings in check, and she outlived 5 of her children and her husband. I don't know how she did it because you can tell having a big family was her prize position. I think I'm like her in that way. I love being a mother and grandmother. Because on my mom's side and dad side it was always about family at least it was back then

My dad and my mom lived together for most of my life and the two together were extremely toxic once the drug and alcohol played a part. Without it both of them were extremely laid back. The thing is as I got older the drugs and alcohol consumed them. It was hard for them to get; they were both known to be hustlers. A Lot of people use the word hustler lightly. My parents were on a different level.

Although my mom may have learned from my had a different

Kind of grind and because of it she attracted some of the biggest drug dealers in Delaware. If they didn't have a heavy drug addiction, then I believe life for us would be extremely different. But their addiction consumed us all. A house of partying and traffic ending in fights. My dad was extremely abusive to my mom when he was high and for years, I saw him beat her badly. Although my mom was one of the toughest women I knew. She was a perfect match for my dad. It was normal for me to see my mom with black eyes or bloody nose. Every day of my life was chaotic. As a young child I remember imagining I was somewhere else. The minute they started getting high and arguing I would imagine being somewhere else where it was peaceful.

I had a friend who lived close to me, and I would
spend a lot of time at her house. It was no secret
what was happening in my household, so I think that
was why her mother allowed me to spend a lot of
time at her house. I just remember how peaceful
their house was and I longed for that kind of peace.
My parents' fights only got worse. As bad as my dad
used to beat my mom, he never laid a hand on us.
He never even raised his voice. My mom was the
disciplinary for the kids and she was strict.
I remember the last fight my parents ever had. My
dad had hurt my mom really bad and finally her
family stepped in. I remember my uncle kicking in
our door to get us away from my dad. After that day,
my mom never went back to him. We went to live
with my Grandmother Ester on my mom's side. It
was a fun time for us. I didn't have to worry about
my mom and dad fighting. The house was crowded
because my grandmother's family from the south

came to live with us. I was in my early teens at this time and big for my age. I started hanging out with my mom's little sister who was then in her early twenties and my cousins who were in their late teens. My life changed drastically. I was going to adult clubs and drinking and smoking cigarettes. My mom was in her own world she

had started to get high and think more but she was still a hustler. Eventually we moved back on the eastside. Although my mom was still stuck once we were back in our own home. I was wild by then and I found ways to do what I wanted to do. I would go over to my aunt's house to watch the kids. I had a lot of freedom over there. I had an older boyfriend and I had to keep it from my mom. I did a respectable job living a double life. By this time, my mom was working for one of the biggest drug dealers in Delaware and she was making him a lot of money. She would have been making a lot of money also, but her addiction had grown and the more she made them thousands of dollars the more she smoked her cut up. Crack cocaine was her drug of choice. It had hit the whole community. Everybody was strung out. Her hustle and addiction caused me to have more freedom. She would always threaten me about what she would do to me if I got pregnant. I was rebellious and unhappy at this time. I was mad at her lifestyle. I was mad at how her and my dad had let drugs consume our life. I was mad that our house was always the hangout house for the drug dealers. I spent most of my time with my new boyfriend who she knew nothing about but before you know it. I did the one thing she told me not to do …. I Got Pregnant

When I asked Na-Shawn to be a part of this project I knew she had a story to tell, but I didn't know how much she had been through. Yes, we grew up together and growing up she was one of my favorite people. As we got older, our lives went in different directions. The best part of her being a part of a project that is so important to me is, I get to know her again. The title of her story made me realize what I admire the most about her. She is literally one of the best mothers I know. A Lot of us had kids at a young age and made many mistakes. I don't see that with Na-shawn. It's like she was born to be an amazing mom. I think that her story will touch a lot of young women. She has accomplished a lot in her life. She's a great friend, cousin, sister, daughter, but you can tell being a mother is her favorite title.

Single Mother

Na-Shawn Lloyd

I am very analytical when it comes to many things. Some people may look for a short answer when being asked a question like, "What is your name? and Where are you from?" Depending on the person who is asking the question or who my audience may be, I may give a 5 second answer or a 5-minute answer. For instance, if I am talking to a stranger or being introduced to a new client (who are particularly youth), I may say "My name is Ms. Lloyd, and I am from Delaware." Short, sweet and to the point.

If I am speaking to someone in a more professional environment, I may get a little more in depth. My name is Na-Shawn Lloyd, M.S. and I was born and raised in Wilmington, Delaware. My mom once told me that my dad wanted to name me LaShawn when I was born. She wasn't having it, because my dad was a tad bit cordial and my mom thought that he may have gotten that name from one of his lady friends, so she gracefully declined. While still willing to compromise she named me Na-Shawn, instead.

Like in many families, you are given nicknames by your close family and friends. Instead of calling me Na-Shawn, those that were closer to me called me Shawn or Shawny. It never really made a difference to me back then because I was a child and these were the people that I loved and cared for, so I embraced it.

Not all of the names that I was called in my childhood were names that I welcomed. I was the youngest of four and two of them were older brothers. They teased me all of the time and called me names like flat head, big feet, and big nose. They were the worst, especially my brother that was right above me. My oldest brother was irking sometimes, but he was more of the protector. I was convinced that the youngest of my brothers' whole existence was to irritate the heck out of me.

We fussed all of the time and fought like cats and dogs. One time we got into a fight, and he busted my lip, and I bloodied his nose. My mom didn't give us beatings, she would just yell and punish us, but this particular time she made us stay in the same room and we couldn't come out until we apologized to each other. We never displayed this kind of behavior on the outside. Despite our sibling rivalry, on the outdoors we were remarkably close and always had each other's backs. The moment we got back home, we were back at each other's necks.

As I got older, I realized that the turmoil that I endured as an adolescent got me ready for the outside world. Those aggravating older brothers that I have, prepared me for the worse. There wasn't anything that anyone could have said that I hadn't already heard. I know that sounds sad, but it's true. Growing up, I was always told that "sticks and stones may break your bones, but names will never hurt you" or "it's not what you are called, it's what you answer to." I get that now, but as a youngster that was easier said than done.

It's very funny, because those same brother's (whom I love dearly may I add) both have big noses. I learned to embrace what some may say are flaws. Many people hate certain parts of their body and mainly because of what other people say or think. Me on the other hand, the older I get the more I love the skin that I am in. This big nose is a Lloyd trait. More than half of the people in my family have big noses. My Grandmother had a big nose, and she was one of the most beautiful, confident, and flyest women I know.

Now the big feet I don't love em,' but I don't hate em.' According to the internet a lot of women my height wear my shoe size and we all know if it's on the internet then it's some truth to it ... Plus, my shoe game is on point, so no one is really worrying about the size of my feet. They are usually admiring the shoes that I have on. As far as the flat head, that comes from my Auntie (my mom's baby sister). She was the sweetest person in the world. I wish I could've been blessed with her beautiful heart but being blessed with any of her physical features is all good.

Last but definitely not least, the most important name that I have been called since the age of seventeen, is mom. Although I love my birth name, there is no better feeling than to be called mom. Being a daughter, sister, aunt, niece, cousin, significant other, best friend, God mom, nothing in this world trumps being a MOM. I'm grateful to God for blessing and entrusting me with my three children. Two girls and a boy to be exact. Well let me clarify that, two young women and a young man. Who are now 29, 23 and 21. My universe in human form. They make my life better; they made me grow up and grow into the woman that I am today.

I used to always say that there is no other name that could hold a candle to the name "mom." Well, that's what I thought, until my grandson came along. I have to be honest, when I was told that my daughter was having a baby, "I wasn't ready." (in my Kevin Hart voice). It wasn't that I didn't think that she was ready or mature enough, she was a 25-year-old college graduate who had already broken the generational curse of teenage pregnancy in our family. I was a teenage mom, my mother, grandmother, great grandmother, and great-great grandmother were all teenage mom's. My daughter has always made me proud; I just wasn't prepared for my baby to grow up. When my grandson was born, we had an immediate connection. Another one of God's many blessings. I knew that when he started talking and called me GG (the name that I preferred that he called me, because I was too young to be anyone's grandmother), that my new name would hold a close second to the undefeated name, Mom. So close, that he would be on their heels. Well, if you knew my grandson you would know that he does things at his own pace and on his own terms. The moment that he finally decided to call me by a name, of all of the different names and abbreviations that children call their Grandparents these days, he decided to call me "Bob." Yes, BOB. No one knew where he got the name from and at first, I was kind of taken aback by it. No matter how many times I tried correcting him, he continued to call me by this name. We couldn't figure it out, but I'm sure he knew the meaning behind it. He was so adamant about calling me Bob, that I finally embraced it and decided to make an acronym out of it. B.O.B, and it stands for Best of Both Worlds. My family thought it was hilarious that he called me this. So much so that his mom (who is a crafter) made me a t-shirt and it says, "It's a hard job being B.O.B, but somebody has to do it." I got comfortable with "Bob" and out of nowhere he started calling me "mom-mom or mom-mom Ashawn." He totally took the first letter off of my name. I guess Bob is one for the books, because if anyone else even jokingly says Bob or anything close to it, he responds "her name is not Bob it's mom-mom."

I was spoiled and highly intelligent, even at a young age. My mother said I used to act mute around strangers, but around my loved ones you couldn't get me to keep quiet. I was the child that would read every billboard that we drove by on a road trip. I was a cry baby. If one of my siblings took the remote, I cried. When my mom would leave and I couldn't tag along, I would cry. If my "other dad" (the man who raised me since I was 3) would leave I would chase the car down the street boohooing, until the car got out of my eyesight. One of my elderly neighbors made a song just for me, because she said every time, she turned around I was crying. Even as I got older and the tears were all dried up, whenever she saw me, she would sing "cry baby cry, stick your finger in your eye tell your mom it wasn't I."

It's funny now, but she used to work my nerves singing that song.

I was very athletic and could beat anybody my age in running, even some of the kids that were older than me. My "other Dad" used to have relay races for the kids in the neighborhood and the winner would get a cash prize. I used to rack up because I was leaving everybody in the dust for those coins. Being a leader and loyalty were two things that I stood by. There weren't many kids my age in my community, so I usually hung around the older kids. Tagging along with my brother and his friends was what I did mainly, until around 4th or 5th grade. That is where my Tomboy stage came to play, running with the boys, wrestling, playing kickball and frisbee. When they jumped on dirty mattresses, climbed gates and trees, threw rocks, blew spit balls and all of those disgusting things that some boys do, is where I drew the line. These were the times that I just hung out with my mom. Which I didn't mind, because back when I was younger my mom was my best friend. We would watch stories like "As The World Turns, Guiding Light and The Young and the Restless." I had no idea what I was watching, but it didn't matter as long as I was there with my mom. It's funny, because still to this day my mom still watches her soap operas, "The Young and the Restless and The Bold and the Beautiful." I catch myself watching it with her from time to time, still asking my many questions and getting irritated when I feel like they are on the same topic for way too long. I could always predict what the outcome would be. I guess that's the writer in me. There was no better moment than hanging out with my mom, or any of my family for that matter.

I was very protective of my family and close friends. A no nonsense type of person. I beat up the bullies. I remember in elementary school this one kid; they called him Big Red because he had this dark red hair. He was such a bully and so disrespectful to the teachers. Everyone enjoyed it when he missed a day of school. He wasn't chubby, but he was thick built with a head the size of a bowling ball. I know it wasn't nice to call people names, because I didn't like when it was done to me. With this kid, you had to stand up for yourself. The more you tried to ignore him, the harder he went on you. He would always throw his weight around because he knew everyone in our grade was afraid of him. I'm not going to say that I was scared of him, but I wasn't about to challenge him to a physical altercation.

I had many fights with my brothers and cousins, but I had never had a fight with someone outside of my family. This particular year I made it as a contestant in the Spelling Bee because I would get A's on my spelling tests. I was book smart, without even trying. My teacher gave out the Spelling Bee words for the finalist to study and of course, I never looked past the first page. I just knew I had it in the bag. I made it to the top four and they asked me to spell a word that I had never heard before and I surely did not know how to spell it. I tried, but I was nowhere close.

 I used to remember the word, because after I got it wrong and lost in the Spelling Bee, I vowed that I would never forget how to spell the word again. Well anyway, I was livid and Big Red with the big head thought that this would be a good day to tease me for losing. I don't know why I allowed him to get under my skin, because he didn't even make it to be able to participate in it. We were getting our jackets to go out for recess, and he kept teasing me for losing and I told him to leave me alone. He got in my face, and I moved around him, he got in my face again and he pushed me. Now why would he do that? We had cubbies for our belongings, and I pushed him so hard, and he fell into the cubby, and I did what I was taught to do. Commenced to tearing his tail up. I got in trouble and wasn't able to go out for recess and my mom got a call, but that was it. Big Red got suspended because that wasn't his first incident. It's safe to say that Big Red with the big head, never messed with me or anybody else in our grade again. Why, may you ask? I'm not sure if it was because he didn't want to take a risk and get beat up again or if it was because he got beat up by a girl. I didn't like to fight, but I wasn't going to back down from one.

I was shy when I got around new people, but it didn't take long for me to make friends. Loyalty and trust were two things that I held in high regard. I loved hard, but I could hold a grudge. My mother took in a few of my friends and family members because of me. Well, she did it because she had a heart of gold, but I told her their situation and she didn't hesitate. I know for a fact that's where I got my caring heart from. I would give anybody the shirt off of my back, but you loss me once you cross me. I can forgive, but I will never forget.

When I was younger, I never envisioned my life as me getting older, having children, and raising them in a one parent household. Yes, my mother was a single mother, and my grandmother was too. I didn't see anything wrong as far as how I grew up, because my life was rather good. My mother worked sometimes two jobs to make ends meet. Did we experience struggles? Absolutely and so did a lot of my friends who came from two parent households. Society tells you that coming from a 2-parent household is what a modeled family is "supposed" to look like. I've learned that everything that looks good isn't good and what you see isn't always what you get. We watched popular television shows growing up that had a husband, a wife, and children.

Then years down the line find out, the characters in those shows weren't what they were portrayed to be and turned out to be a bunch of "characters" in their real life. No doubt they were just tv shows, but I know I'm not the only one who watched these shows and thought this is how my life was going to be. Real life imitates art, right?

Of course, I wanted my children to be raised with both parents. Single parenthood was not in my radar. I always knew that I would be married in a house on the hills, with a white picket fence. My childhood sweetheart and I were together since I was in the 1st grade, and he was in the 2nd. I know you are probably thinking, how are you in a relationship in the 1st and 2nd grade? Well, we were. We grew up in the same community and our families were close knit. It started out as "puppy love," but it was love. The older we got, the more time we spent together, the stronger our bond became. There wasn't anything that we wouldn't do for each other. We went from loving each other, to also being in love with each other. Imagine J and Bee or Russell and C. Better yet, Michelle and Barack. Yeah, I'm going a little too far with the last one, but you get the picture.

We talked about marriage and children all of the time. People that were older than us admired our relationship and it was great, until it wasn't. I am not going to sit up here and pretend like things were peaches and cream every waking moment. Or act as if we didn't have some trials and tribulations because we did. A lot of those problems started, when he realized he wanted to hang out in the streets. Outside of our relationship, I had my own dreams and aspirations. I was going to graduate high school and go to college to become a social worker (I had the mindset that I wanted to "Save the World"). Plus, my mother and I conversed about this all of the time. She would always say to me, "you are going to college" and I knew by any means necessary, I was going to make that happen and eventually I did. I received my Associates and Bachelor's in Criminal Justice; my Master's in Administration in Human Services and I am currently 1 class away from my second Master's in Organizational Leadership. But that's a little further down in my Single Motherhood, let's get back to how I became..." A Single Mother." Now where did I leave off? Oh, I didn't have time for that "street life." I let him go about his way and I went my way. He had a certain swag about him that attracted a lot of females. Now that he was into the street life and getting a little coin, the chickens came out of the coop. I didn't approve of him hanging out, but I wasn't about to let these groupies snatch up the young man that was destined to be my husband. It was only right that I went back and reclaimed what was mine. We got back together, and I set some ground rules and I quote "don't ever bring anything that you do in the streets around me or near me. The people that you associate with in that lifestyle, don't bring them around me either." Mind you, we are children, trying to do grownup things. If I knew then what I know now, I would've done nothing differently, I know you may have thought I was going to say the "politically correct" thing, but no sir and no ma'am. I don't regret anything that I ever did in life. If I would've changed even one thing my children would not be who they are.

Now let's carry on. By this time, we were all in, and I mean ALL IN. We were inseparable. One day I was using the restroom and my stomach started hurting really bad and a huge glob of blood came out of me and fell in the toilet. I had no idea what it was, and I was terrified. I picked it up out of the toilet (thoroughly washed my hands of course) and took it to the emergency with me. Yup, honey I sure did. I didn't know what it was, my friend didn't know and neither did the boyfriend. But I know who would know, "the doctor." He got us a ride to the hospital and while I was in the waiting room, I saw my mom's cousin. He asked what I was doing there, and I told him that I wasn't feeling well. He asked where my mom was, because he knew very well that she would have been there. I told him that I wasn't sure. One thing about my family: they know how to run their mouths, so I knew this was going to get out. I can hear him now, "you know Na-Shawn, her little boyfriend and one of her girlfriends were at the emergency room." He was flamboyant, so just imagine...lol. I loved my cousin so much, but baby he knew he could keep something going.

Before I could blink my eye, my mother was at the hospital. My first thought was dang, bad news travels fast, but that wasn't the case. Due to me being a minor, the hospital had to contact my next of kin. I found out that I had a miscarriage, and I didn't need a D&C (dilation and curettage). That is a surgical procedure that is sometimes done after a female has a miscarriage to remove any remaining tissue. In my case, the miscarriage had already flowed naturally. To say I was scared was an understatement. One, my Momma was upset with all three of us. Me, my boyfriend, and my poor friend. Two, I know it only takes one time, but dang your girl just started having sex and I get pregnant. My momma wanted better for me. I felt horrible for disappointing her. On the flip side, to find out that I was pregnant and lost it had me and the boyfriend heartbroken. We were lectured by our family, but that didn't matter to us. We were in love and as foolish as it was, we vowed to have another baby and soon. This time it will be planned.

My mom wasn't about to let that go down again, because she took me to the gynecologist and put me on birth control immediately. She scolded us about being too young to be doing the things that we were doing and stated we weren't ready to take on such a huge responsibility. Putting me on contraception wasn't her giving us a free pass to go buck wild. She was a realist and she rather had been safe than sorry. Been there and done that, a few times and she was not about to sit around and watch the same thing happen to me.

I started the pill, and it messed my cycle up. It felt like I was on my menstrual for a whole month straight. I've had my period since the age of twelve. They have never been this irregular and it was depressing. I went to my next appointment and my gynecologist said that this is how it is in the beginning and once my body gets used to them, I will see a change. Well, it didn't change, and I stopped taking them. Of course, my Mom wasn't aware that I wasn't taking them because she may have laid a helping hand on the both of us.

He wasn't going to school, and he didn't have a job. I didn't approve of it because I wanted better for him. He was street savvy, me on the other hand was still going to school and getting good grades. I was on the track team and the fastest girl on the team, might I add. He would come to some of my track meets, when he could pay someone to use their car and no, he didn't have a driver's license.

Most of the time after the track meet, I would catch the athletic bus home. On this particular day, we had a track meet at the school. It was earlier in the meet, and I started to feel sick. After I ran my first event, I could not move another muscle, I was in excruciating pain. Just so happens the after-school bus hadn't left yet, and my track Coach told me to go home. When I got on the bus, the bus driver asked what was wrong and I told him that my stomach was killing me. He replied, "You aren't pregnant, are you?" That hadn't crossed my mind, but I immediately responded, "No."

I got to my stop, which was quite a way from my house. I walked home and called one of my friends. She had already had a baby, so I figured she would probably know if the pain I was experiencing could be pregnancy pain. She wasn't sure because she hadn't had the pain that I described. She went and got me two home pregnancy tests from the Dollar Store. That's what I said, the Dollar Store. She had taken them before, and she said they were accurate. I took test number one, positive. My instant response was, "this can't be right!" She responded matter of factly, "Oh it's right." Although I believed her, I had to take the second one and lo and behold, it was the same. "You got to be freaking kidding me!" I shouted. My emotions were all over the place. It had to be like 3 or 4 months since my miscarriage and I ended up pregnant again. "You Big Dummy" in my Fred Sanford voice. The first person I thought of was my mother. She was going to have a conniption. The rest is a blur. I can't remember if I called the boyfriend, or if I waited for him to come in. What I do know is, I didn't get any sleep that night. I cried and he cried because I was crying. He didn't play about me and hated to see me upset. Even though we said this is what we wanted, now that it had happened, I wasn't too sure. I was smarter than this. I was one of the fastest girls in the State (as a sophomore) and an honor roll student. Those tears of regret lasted but a moment. Once the initial shock wore off, we were ecstatic. I believe he was happier than I was, and I loved him for that. This was the person that I gave my virginity to, the man that I was supposed to grow old with. What he lacked, I provided and vice versa. If we could've gotten married at a tender age, I'm sure we would have. We knew our love for each other could withstand anything. No matter what, we were having this baby and we were going to love it more than we loved ourselves.

All of our close friends knew about the pregnancy. We weren't sure when we would tell my mother, but I knew it wasn't going to be any time soon. I was small in size, and the baby was filling me up in all the right places, so it was hard to tell. I started wearing bigger clothing and stayed out of the presence of my mother and two older siblings as much as possible. I knew if my sister or older brother found out, it was over. The younger of my brothers wouldn't tell because I've held many of his secrets. Even the one with him getting someone pregnant the year prior. A few months went by, and I almost let the cat out of the bag. A friend of mine needed some sanitary napkins and I told her that I had some for her. While I was getting them out of the closet, my Mom asked me how I was giving away my pads when I was going to need them for myself? My friend intervened and stated that she would replace them when her Aunt got home. She saved me at that moment, but I knew I had to tell my mother soon.

Keeping something so special from my family was starting to get to me and I had to tell somebody, so I thought my aunt (my mom's baby sister who was all of our favorite) was that person. She assured me that my secret was safe with her. I thought that to be true until we were in the line at the grocery store getting food for my nieces first birthday party, which was also my mother's birthday. While in line my mom turned around to me and asked, "What are you going to do with a baby?" I was totally caught off guard and the only thing I could do was hunch my shoulders and say, "I don't know." If my mother were going to chastise me, she wouldn't have started this conversation in a grocery store line. She just wanted me to know that she knew. At this moment, a weight was lifted off of my shoulder. I thought about my aunt, and I chuckled. She adored her big sister, so I don't even know why I expected her to keep a secret of such magnitude from her. I was happy that she told her.

That next week my mom made me an appointment with an Obstetrician. Come to find out I was 6 months pregnant. My mother advised us both of how crucial keeping this secret from her could've become. No prenatal care for 6 months could have been very harmful to our baby. To God be the Glory, our baby was doing well.

Pressing forward again, we had a beautiful baby girl. This was the happiest day of our lives. I had her early in the morning and he was at the hospital all day and all night long. He thought that he would be able to be slick and stay over, but the nurse came in after visiting hours was over and told him that he had to go. Even then he didn't leave, he said security was going to have to come and escort him out. I didn't want him to cause a scene, so I told him to leave and come back in the morning. He held his daughter again, cried and then left.

The next day I heard someone come in and I thought that it was my daughter's Father, but it wasn't. To my surprise, it was my dad (my biological Father). Come to find out his sister was a Nurse in the Labor and Delivery Department and she saw my name on the clipboard. She never came in, but she contacted my Dad to let him know that his oldest daughter had a baby. The most astounding part of his visit wasn't that he was there, but that he was sober. Every encounter that I can remember with my Dad, he was under the influence of alcohol. I've seen pictures when I was a baby and he wasn't intoxicated, but I was too young to remember those times. So, for him to show up after I've just given birth and during one of the happiest moments of my life, meant the world to me. All of the other times that he didn't show up, no longer mattered.

My mom was very protective and didn't allow anyone to come around her children with any confusion. I know, that's where I got it from. My mother never had any ill will towards my dad, and she never talked bad about him. She allowed me to see who he was for myself. My mom would always say that he was a good person, despite his abuse of alcohol. From this day on my dad and I relationship grew. He had become a part of every milestone of my life and for that I am forever grateful. I included this part, because who else is better to insert other than the man who contributed to my mom being a Single Mother.

After I was released from the hospital (7 days later),
my life changed drastically. That school year I had
started going to a school for pregnant girls, which
was helpful because everyone around me was a
teenage mom. I was one of the last people to have
my baby and it seemed like I was pregnant forever.
Once I had my daughter, I had an option to bring her
to school with me or leave her at home with my
sister or my cousin (who lived across the yard from
us). I opted to keep my baby home, because how
they cared for the babies in that daycare was not up
to my standards. The boyfriend wasn't working or
going to school, but he didn't have enough
experience watching newborn's to keep our baby all
day. That probably wasn't an option anyway
because he couldn't stay out of the streets long
enough. We had a baby now and we couldn't do the
things that we used to do. I got it, but he clearly

didn't. Sometimes you don't know how you will react to a situation until it smacks you in the face. My tolerance for foolishness was lower. People started coming back telling me all kinds of stuff. Said he was cheating and doing drugs, very harsh drugs. Once we became parents, it was time to put away all of those childish, irresponsible things. I guess he missed that memo. I didn't believe the drug rumor and it wasn't because I was in denial. He was still getting money and I had seen people who were high before, and I never saw him under the influence. The moment I knew the rumors were true, is when one day we were having a conversation and his nose started bleeding out of nowhere. I wasn't only disappointed; I was disgusted, and it was a wrap. It hurt, but I was not about to allow someone who uses drugs to be around me or my daughter. This person that I loved and thought that I knew, was clearly fighting some demons that I had no knowledge of. He loved me and his daughter without question, the problem was he didn't love himself.

Single Mother

By: Na-Shawn Lloyd

Am I a Single Mother because my marital status
is single…since I never married?

Or is it because their father's didn't bother, so I

Doubled Down on these kids that I carried.

Being a Single Mother, wasn't all that it's
cracked up to be.

I had other dreams; this life wasn't for me.

OR was it?

Single Mom's come a dime a dozen.

Don't believe me, give me a moment…while I
ask my mom & my cousin.

Then again, I ain't got nothing to prove.

Their loss, I didn't lose.

I wear this single mom stamp, like a champ.

Couldn't walk a mile in my shoes.

No pats on the back. No need for reinforcement
Or validation.

When it comes to my kids, I'm jumping
hurdles/overcoming any obstacles I'm facing.

No bitterness, No envy.

I put myself in situations where I compromised
my integrity.

So, I had to bite the bullet, couldn't let them be
the death of me.

I Learned Lessons for the sake of my 3 Blessings.

This was written. It's how it was *supposed* to be.

No questions, No second guessing. They Deserve
to get the BEST VERSION OF ME!!

-*A Single Mother*

www.ingramcontent.com/pod-product-compliance
Lightning Source LLC
Chambersburg PA
CBHW060926030726
47503CB00003B/496